CTHULHU: A LOVE STORY

JC RUDKIN

FyreSyde
publishing

CHAPTER 1

The waters near the beach roiled fiercely.

At first, it had only been a rogue wave or two, seemingly larger and more aggressive than its watery sisters. Soon one or two became three became four became a dozen; then it looked as if the sea itself was boiling.

Fish rolled helplessly on its restless surface. A few fish threw themselves at the beach, flopping and gasping. Sand churned in the waters, but no heat came from it. I watched with rapt attention to see where this was going, as I'd seen a similar phenomenon before, but none quite this intense. I was almost positive the boil was an illusion of sorts and likely not the last I'd see today if I stayed by the beach, but I couldn't take the chance that it was just a trick of the ocean. If something really was coming for me, I needed to not get caught.

Years of paranoia, bolstered by my study of occult texts and knowledge of dangerous, supernatural entities in this universe, had refined my instinct for self-preservation. This illusion could be a precursor to something very, very bad coming out of the ocean, and I was still at least a quarter-mile from my home. The same ocean that drew me to its side to write now made me uneasy. I watched the growing waves as I tucked my tablet into my beach bag.

I bolted.

Like a signal to my tormentor, jets of water shot up from the beach. Straight streams released like fire hoses, each one seemingly random but closing in behind me, violent puffs of sand spewing with each eruption when I glanced back. I ran faster, heart pumping like it was fit to burst. I was a writer, not an athlete, and I worried this unexpected sprint would kill me as surely as that which pursued me.

I turned into the little arch off the beach, intricately woven with grapevines and decorated with seashells, and started up the stone path toward my house. I realized the sounds of the approaching water had stopped, and I finally turned to look and catch my breath.

I thought I could see tentacles just beneath the now docile waves, hovering, waiting. I stood a moment longer, absent-mindedly rubbing the miniature nautilus pendant that had bounced out of my tank top. Once my heart rate was under control, I turned and headed up the stairs that lead from the beach to my backyard. Plodding up, with occasional glances back over my shoulder at the water, I finally convinced myself I was safe. Still, my relief was palpable when I opened the French double doors and stepped into my sunroom. I closed the door behind me with a sigh of gratitude for the feeling of safety.

Had it been real? Was any of this real? I couldn't tell. I wondered if my mind was finally slipping like my mother's already had, or if this was the result of something inside me, buried in my DNA, that was pushing me toward a destiny I did not want. I felt a headache coming on, a deep throb in both temples like a marching drumbeat.

I carefully removed my tablet and set it on the counter, rubbing my hand over its protective case to reassure myself that it was, and I was, okay. I poured myself a healthy glass of

Maker's Mark to calm my nerves and retreated to my living room where I could overlook the sea from a safe distance. I dared only to venture out as far as the deck, just outside, but left the door open for a hasty retreat, if necessary.

It felt like the whole world had gone mad in the last few years. Chaotic weather, chaotic governments, violence, and fear across the globe. Admittedly, this had been great for my book sales because it seemed everyone wanted to escape into my made-up world of horrors, where the heroine prevailed after 300 or so pages, but it hadn't been good for humanity. Heroines with fictional skills just weren't enough. World events were reaching a crescendo.

I knew I was likely one of the few people on the planet who suspected the truth.

Cultists had set this monstrosity of a timeline into motion, although they had failed in reaching their ultimate goal – the destruction of civilization. They were a death cult, calling their horrible god into the world to wreak havoc without consequence. They were also just mad enough to think that their status as his summoners would elevate them to kings of the ruins, ruling at the side of their mad deity, instead of becoming devout ashes beneath his tread.

Quite simply, they fucked up.

They birthed their god into the world in human form, then failed to control it. They stashed the supernatural faculties of that corruption into a stone gate for safekeeping and went to work on the confused human they created. They experimented on it, trying to enrage it, trying to engage it. Trying to reunite it with its own rightful power. In the process, they created a powerful entity.

Then they tried to use me to stuff that genie back into the bottle.

Goddamn idiots.

I reached down to pull up my pendant and traced its irregular whorls, as I so often did to comfort myself or just to think. So much cosmic power contained in such a delicate package. In fifteen years, it had never again betrayed its might, its capacity for world destruction. But it could again, at any time. It didn't belong in this world any longer, and truly, it never did. And I was the only one who could remove it from this world and lock it away in another.

I looked out over the ocean as I gently stroked the little shell, feeling my connection to it, to the faint pulse of power within it. Between the soothing motion of my fingertips on the nautilus and the Maker's Mark, I could feel my headache receding. But that energy and alcohol weren't going to take me much further. It was time to confront a prophecy that predicted my failure to be my own person. A prophecy foretelling the end of humanity, and me a part of it.

A prophecy I did not want.

Now with fifteen years of research, work, and practice, I could read the signs. I knew the stars were aligning to fix cosmic mistakes made long ago, but it would take someone who understood the stakes and the powers involved to intervene and avoid Armageddon.

I didn't want to be that person. I just wanted my life back.

I also realized, with each water spout, with each geyser spewing up from the beach, with each rogue wave dashing onto the rocks beneath my house, that something else wanted my life as well. I could no longer bide my time and hope no need for a decision would come to pass. The stars would be in position in another two days, and that could be my only chance.

It was time to put an end to this madness. First thing in the morning, I would start the journey that would reveal my destiny – short on physical mileage, long on cabalistic utility. But first, I needed to make one last pass through my notes – copious research into dark magics most people didn't know existed in our world. And if I was going to head down this shadowy path, I was going to need fortification and sustenance.

I ordered delivery of my two favorite pizzas and a six-pack of local brew, a rare indulgence for me, and settled in for a final evening of study and planning. If I was going to retake my life, I had to put planning into practice. I gathered and organized notes on spells and rituals, spending extra time on the ones devoted to opening and closing portals to other worlds.

I reviewed histories of various cults and supernatural entities to refresh my memory. I went to the pantry where I kept all manner of spell components and supernatural ingredients for performing rituals that most people believed were folk tales and fairy stories. I designed my pantry to be an armory for fighting dark legends too scary to be true.

But I knew they were real.

And they were coming to New Jersey in two days.

And I was the only one who could stop them.

I awoke the next morning with a kink in my neck from falling asleep on my notebooks. Although I was feeling a little achy from lack of sleep, I was also feeling invigorated because it was time to put my plans into motion

Which is how I found myself, a few hours later, stepping off the 1 Train at South Ferry Subway Station with the rest of the crush of New Yorkers and everyday tourists eagerly looking around while clutching their purses. Hustling out into the mid-afternoon sunshine, I walked into the Battery, breaking from the commuters who headed to the Staten Island Ferry's Whitehall Terminal.

Although I was on a mission of sorts, I took a few minutes to step inside and walk through the gardens in the park. Being late Spring, a riot of color greeted me. I breathed deep, enjoying the scents of the many flowers mixed with just a tinge of dampness from New York Harbor just outside the door. Despite the visual stimulus, the garden was an oasis of calm, a place where I could order my mind and prepare for the assault that would surely be coming my way.

I caught myself absently rubbing my pendant, as I often did when I was nervous. The nautilus shell on my chain was beautiful to me, even in its deformity. Its logarithmic spiral distorted by odd whorls, lending it a wonky and somewhat disturbing appearance. The kind of thing you don't notice at first glance but that you can't avoid once you see it. Not as Nature intended. I knew that if I looked closely at some of the flowers in the Battery, especially the sunflowers, I would likely see the same. The corruption was local, and it was subtle, but anyone would find instances of this all over the tri-state coastal region, as well as north into the shorelines of Rhode Island and Massachusetts if they took the time to look.

When I knew I couldn't put off my task any longer, I walked back outside and over to the dock area where I could get the best view of the harbor. The crowds for the Ferry were far to my left, and the water stretched out before me. Mercifully, there were fewer tourists out today. I already felt guilty about the horror to which I was about to subject them, but it had to be done. If I could act as a conduit for some of the latent powers in my pendant, I could perhaps mitigate some of the damage. But I needed the real power -- the raw, unbridled, feral power of the pendant – to get my life back. And I needed to call the evil to me instead of letting it catch me in its own time, even if that involved all of these people.

As selfish as it was, I had to try.

Besides, New Yorkers seemed to be a resilient group. They could handle it.

I'm sure I was quite a sight, wheeling my Louis Vuitton weekend luggage onto the docks. It didn't really go with the casual look I'd curated for the event – crisp blue jeans, sensible shoes, and my old NYU sweatshirt. Of course, my luggage did match my handbag, but the contents of my purse weren't something I think you would find in the bag of the average New York.

Setting it atop my luggage, I took out homemade sidewalk chalk infused with sand from the beach by my home; sea salt evaporated from the Pacific Ocean; seaweed from three beaches near Providence, Rhode Island; and a few cones of frankincense that I enjoyed as much for the scent as the protection. Finally, I set a small bag by my feet, its festive tiki design a contrast to my otherwise metaphysically weighty components. Closing my eyes, I tried to clear my mind so I could remember all of the steps to the ritual, as well as block out the stares of the tourists who were probably wondering what this weirdo was doing when there was a perfectly good view of the Statue of Liberty to enjoy right there in front of her.

Gathering my supplies, first, I drew an elder sign on the dock large enough to accommodate me and my luggage. I never knew if I was being followed by cultists, so I was always better safe than sorry with my warding. The people in my vicinity probably walked around my space without realizing why or even really seeing me. Second, I made another smaller elder sign at my feet with the pieces of seaweed, set the frankincense within it, and lit the small globs of sap afire. When they burned down to a glowing ember, a comforting fog filled the confines of my space, an elder sign-shaped column of fragrant smoke wafting ever upward. I was as prepared as I could possibly be for the unexpected. Finally, I clutched my pendant tight and began to chant.

At first, nothing seemed to happen, and I questioned whether I was pronouncing everything correctly. It's not like there was a Duolingo module on ancient alien languages, so I could only pronounce words as they appeared in writing and hope for the best.

But then, I could feel the air turn, dropping at least 30 degrees and reeking of death, even through my incense.

People near me began milling around in odd patterns, totally unaware of their own actions. Once again, the ocean roiled, and water shot up in powerful columns, soaking everything around me. Fish threw themselves onto the dock, panicking some in the crowd, while other people pounced on the helpless fish and devoured them alive, further horrifying the remaining onlookers.

The mayhem crept inexorably closer to me as I continued my chant. When I thought my voice was going to break from the strange syllables and unearthly tones I produced, I finally saw him.

A huge figure emerged from the waves, its tentacled head breaking the water first, followed by its immense bulk, grasping clawed hands, and tattered, spike-tipped wings. The creature, a god really, towered over the Statue of Liberty and strode past it like any other New Yorker making their way down the sidewalk toward work. It stopped mid-harbor, threw its horrible head back, tentacles stretching in all directions, and let loose a cry so fierce, and yet still so wretched, that most of the people in the milling crowd dropped to their knees, wailing and clawing at the ground like rabid animals.

The beast resumed its stroll through the New York Harbor, stopping briefly to bend down and glare into a boat or push it aside as a beach wader might do to various bit of flotsam around their thighs as they walked the surf. I stopped my chant, but it did not halt its progress forward. Its walk was slow and casual, with not a care for the pandemonium its very existence was causing.

I thought it would come straight to me, to my call, but instead, it moved past me. Not 200 yards to my left, it walked right up to Whitehall Terminal and peered into the building. It braced itself on the viewing platform and gazed at the queued-up passengers, dark red eyes unblinking. Dozens of people screamed and scrambled for safety. Some instead stood trans-fixed, watching their approaching death calmly, disconnected already from this mortal coil. A very few others dropped to their knees, prostrating themselves before the horrendous monstrosity, their minds snapping but also recognizing an ancient rhythm that demanded their worship, their obsequiousness.

Then it turned, looked down, and saw me.

I stood on the platform outside in the now chilly day and faced down the horror. It didn't have the power to frighten me, not anymore, not after 15 years of always looking over my shoulder. Spreading my arms out wide, I shouted into the maelstrom with all the intensity I could muster.

"Ryley! I can't talk to you when you're like this! Come to me. Please."

And I meant it literally. I could not talk to him when he was like this. His was an alien intelligence that could not connect with humanity at all.

Not in this form.

In what felt like the blink of an eye, the horror in the sea was gone, disappeared, and he stood before me now, as a man – a young, handsome man I had forgotten how much I missed. As he walked across the dock toward me, the ward of protection in which I was standing burned to nothing, leaving me defenseless. All the protective smoke around me wafted away on a gentle breeze, as ephemeral as the chaos that had disappeared in an instant. Although his clothes were already dry, he shook out his still-damp hair with a tantalizing toss of his head, which somehow dried it completely. Involuntarily, I sucked in a quick breath.

"Morningstar," he barely breathed, his eyes blinking rapidly to adjust to his transformation and the light of day. As he blinked, his eyes shifted from that hideous, monstrous red to a cool, stunning aquamarine that seemed almost the more unnatural color.

I hadn't heard his pet name for me in nearly fifteen years. It still set off chords in my body that thrummed to his particular frequency. It also set off a flutter of panic now that I knew the truth behind the name.

I watched him closely. He stretched his back. He flexed his hands, alternating between clenching and unclenching his fists and waving his fingers, watching them as a newborn baby might. He rolled his shoulders and neck in one of his old habits I recognized, making his longer hair shimmer in the light.

After a few moments, he finally smiled. "It's so good to see you again."

Once in his human form, the crowds around us slowly came to their senses, already processing and repressing the memories of the horror that had just befallen them. Before I could ask the questions that brought me to this time and place, I clutched at my pendant and began a new chant. I could feel it drain from my own mental reserves, sending sharp spikes of pain through my head, but it had to be done. It was a chant of healing and forgetfulness, peace and abstraction, meant to scrape away every detail and memory of the summoning. I cast the spell out as far around me as I was able. People who witnessed this horror would go on about their days, sanity intact, and let slip from their minds everything that happened in the last few minutes.

It was the only mercy I had available to bestow, and I gave it willingly.

When I finished, he looked at me anew.

"Still thinking of others." He smirked. "A novel concept, and one I still confess to not understanding after all this time. You don't know any of these people, do you?"

"They're people. They don't deserve this."

"They're people, Morningstar. Of course, they deserve this." He waved dismissively at the docks, at the ferry terminal, then smiled again, radiant in the sunlight as the air rewarmed around us. "But you don't."

"I need a favor, Ryley," I said, stumbling a little over his name. He had been so long away. I'd ceased to think of him as human anymore, which, I guess, he really wasn't. I was older, even had a little grey in my hair, and he was still the young college student I'd fell in love with a lifetime ago. I wasn't sure he could look any other way.

"Let me look at you first." He walked to me and held me by my upper arms, smiling. He lifted one hand to run a finger delicately down my jawline. "It hasn't been long, but I'd already forgotten how your skin felt." He inhaled deeply, "How very warm you smelled. Mmm."

Any self-consciousness on my part melted away under his gaze.

His eyes locked onto mine in a way that was both terrifying and thrilling for me. "And how beautiful your eyes were, like emeralds pulled from the Spanish galleons at the bottom of the ocean. I'd always promised you I would show you those, the exact two emeralds I was thinking of whenever I saw you. They're actually not too far from where you were born."

His voice poured over me, warm and familiar. Memories of nights listening to him tell me about wonders in the ocean I'd never thought to see. Stories I had thought were fanciful fictions. I was so wrong.

He smiled again, probably looking a bit like a besotted suitor to an outsider, but I clearly saw the predatory gleam in his eyes.

By this time, almost every person on the dock and in the Battery had resumed their lives as if nothing had happened. I was grateful for that. I wasn't sure how the folks in Brooklyn or Jersey City had fared through the episode, but there was only so much I could do. Despite the typical crush of tourists, we had a spacious chunk of the dock to ourselves. Even though no one seemed to notice us, everyone avoided us, and no one made eye contact of any sort. We were invisible but still influencing our surroundings, still giving people that prescient tingle in the backs of their necks. That primitive warning of danger had alerted us since before the beginning of humanity.

We stood, inches apart, in our cursed unity, utterly separate from that humanity.

Tentatively, he reached for me. I didn't move. I should have been terrified but was more curious than anything.

As he caressed my face with the barest brush of his fingertips, his hand strayed down my neck and touched the chain of my necklace. He snapped back his hand like he'd touched a live wire.

"Protection in place?"

"Always."

He briefly spread his hands in a non-threatening gesture, then reached for me again. He lightly stroked my cheek with the back of his fingers, gazing at me like he was reliving a lifetime of memories. Then he stopped and just stared directly into my eyes. It became uncomfortable.

"It's been a long time, Ry."

"Has it really?"

"Almost fifteen years."

He shook his head, breaking the spell that held us both nearly immobile. "Just a blink for me. Not even a cat nap."

I flinched, knowing what he meant, the accusation in his voice.

"And now you need a favor. You know you only need ask. Flood New York City? Drown a continent? Anything for you, my dear."

"Remove the madness."

He tsked, clicking his tongue a few times like he was relearning the human gesture. "Oooh, that's a big ask. It's so much easier to flood a few islands, eat a few cultists, you know." He waved dismissively.

I pulled my pendant out from my shirt, and his unnaturally clear aquamarine eyes snapped to it. "I can pay."

"Pay? Why, Amanda, no need to be that way. You know I could never say no to you."

Hearing my name rumble from him in that deep timbre of his thrilled me more than I expected.

Unable to help myself, I dropped my pendant back into my shirt, enjoying watching his eyes drop with it. Brazenly, I stepped into the space between us and kissed him. He tasted like the sea, cool breezes with a salty bite. I wound my hands into his thick black curls and felt his arms pull me tighter, one hand pushing into the small of my back. I could devour him whole. I had missed him so much. I heard him groan a little and knew I had to stop before we both were lost.

I slowly and reluctantly drew away, my body aching for more.

"I'd forgotten the benefits of humanity." He kissed me once again, lightly this time. "And the drawbacks." He shifted uncomfortably in his ever-present faded blue jeans. "I've missed both. And I thank you for the reminder."

CHAPTER 2

A Little More Than 20 Years Ago

S ummer days in Florida along the Gulf of Mexico are a contradiction if you're a teenager.

Expectation is in the air. It smells like sunshine and coconut-scented tanning lotion. There are plenty of jobs available for those willing to work. The beach is never far, and the water beckons you and your friends to come and have a great time. Magic is a part of your world like a summer-long trip to Disney.

Desperation is in the air. It smells like overheated asphalt and fryer oil that should have been changed three shifts ago. Those available jobs? Usually minimum wage, or under-the-table subminimum, for crowds of short-armed tourists − bossy, demanding, rarely tipping because this-place-is-way-more-expensive-than-I-thought-it-would-be   or   we-don't-do-that-where-I'm-from tourists. The beach is crowded, as there is no longer an off-season in Florida, and the oppressive heat weighs down everything from your hair to your soul. It's hurricane season. Sometimes, you only have a three-day window to be ready for a storm to rip apart your home and decimate your town.

It was in this push and pull of a Florida summer that Amanda graduated from high school. She wasn't yet 18, but she had her diploma, a full-ride scholarship to NYU, and two years in at a part-time job at her local bookstore. And like a Florida summer, Amanda's life was quite the dichotomy. She was caught in the no-man's-land between her past and her future, not really a kid anymore and not yet an adult on her own.

Having a financially insecure childhood already drove Amanda to be self-sufficient in all ways. She had to have her mom co-sign to open a savings account, but then she saved meticulously. Her only splurge was a new book each month and sometimes a fancy journal or pen, everything purchased with her employee discount. The only thing more important to her than financial security was her creative writing, which she knew, even at a young age, was a sucker's play. She didn't want to be starving, but she did want to be an artist.

Last year, she actively worked to make her dreams reality. She studied hard and was planning on going to Pensacola Junior College – if she could get good financial aid – or to the University of Florida – if she could land a full-ride scholarship. She applied for federal financial aid and struggled to explain the origins of her mom's only source of income: a check each month from an unknown benefactor who was likely Amanda's father or his family. She couldn't supply the other half of her family's income information because she had no idea who her father was. Without paperwork her mother couldn't or wouldn't provide, she was left unable to qualify for standard financial aid. Undaunted, she applied for every scholarship she could find and put her name into common application scholarship pools. She wrote essays and letters, and even a poem once, in her quest to land college money. Using application fee waivers and some money she had saved up for this purpose, she applied to many schools.

What Amanda really wanted was to go to New York and become a famous novelist, but she couldn't possibly save enough money for that. Still, several New York City and East Coast schools were among the many to which she applied as a concession to her ambitions. She had to keep that dream alive. She even applied to every Ivy League school east of the Mississippi in hopes of hitting that jackpot.

By February, her efforts began to pay off. She won a small scholarship from a local civic organization and received notification that she got a 100% tuition waiver for a local college. But that meant living at home, which wasn't an ideal situation. She was accepted by several of the universities to which she applied, although no others offered her scholarships that would make attendance possible. She received rejection letters from all of the Ivies.

Then, one grey day in late April, she came home from her afterschool job and received what she came to think of as "The Letter" in the mail. Upon opening it, Amanda discovered she was the recipient of the prestigious Baratarian Order Scholarship. Awarded to a distinguished young scholar of merit, it covered room and board at the university of the student's choice for up to five years, as long as the recipient maintained a 3.0-grade point average. She turned up her stereo and danced with unbridled joy, turning the small apartment into her own personal club. She was elated at her amazing luck.

That was the day her world changed.

Amanda put together a small, celebratory dinner, breaking out the Corelle dishware instead of paper plates and pulling out two mismatched wine glasses from the back of the cupboard. She made spaghetti with meat sauce from a jar and filled the glasses with cherry Kool-Aid. It felt very fancy.

It felt considerably less fancy when she ended up eating alone after her mom didn't make it home by early evening. Resigned, she put the leftovers in the fridge and cleaned up the dishes. When her mom, Caroline, came home later that night, Amanda was on the couch reading a book, her treat from her last paycheck.

"I'm home," was all her mom said as she wandered into the kitchen and opened the fridge to rummage around. She pulled out the plate of spaghetti wrapped in plastic wrap and popped it into the microwave for a few minutes.

"This sauce from a jar or a can?" she asked.

"Jar," Amanda replied.

"I like the canned stuff better," Caroline mumbled, getting the green can of Parmesan from the counter. When her plate was ready, she dumped about a quarter of the can onto it and started shoveling it into her mouth while standing over the sink.

Amanda felt her ire rising. She waited until Caroline had finished off her meal with an outsized belch and set her plate in the sink before she spoke again. Amanda had hoped to tell her mother her good news over a nice dinner and make a fuss over it. She had dreamed it would be a happy occasion. She should have known better. Instead, her mother ruined her plans yet again.

Amanda set down her book, stood to catch her mother as she exited the kitchen, and made her announcement.

"I got a full-ride scholarship. I'm going to New York University in the fall."

It was like Amanda rang the bell at the start of a boxing match, and she and her mom were the top bout on the card. It was on.

"You can't just leave Pensacola, for God's sake! You can't just pack up and leave me, leave the state," her mom said. "After everything I have done for you. Everything I have given up to raise you." The explosion was immediate. Caroline went from zero to sixty in record time.

Amanda felt her temper rising, as it often did when she tried to talk to her mother. Her mom was barely 15 years older than Amanda, and sometimes it felt to Amanda like arguing with a stubborn older sister, except they had no parent to referee their matches. Biting retorts jumped to the forefront of her mind – *Everything what, Mom? Let me make my own dinner? Do all my own laundry and yours? Be left alone for days at a time? Make me do my homework by myself?* -- held only barely in check by her tightly pursed lips. She took a few deep breaths as her mom stared at her, awaiting an answer.

"Which is why I would think you would want the best for me."

"You can't afford New York. It's unbelievably expensive. And you don't even know how to survive on your own. What will you do without me?"

About half the housework was Amanda's immediate and uncharitable thought.

"My expenses are covered by a scholarship," was the half-truth Amanda opted to use. It was just room and board, but her mom didn't really understand college or college costs. Her mom dropped out of high school when she got pregnant with Amanda. She hadn't been around when Amanda was doing the research on colleges because she hadn't cared about it.

"And who gave you this money?"

"I told you. I got a scholarship. It's the Baratarian Order Scholarship. I am this year's Distinguished Young Scholar of Merit."

"I've never even heard of them."

"Mom, I applied for a lot of scholarships," Amanda hedged. She hadn't actually heard of them either. "Some of the common applications cover dozens of them. But what is important is that I have the money to go to college."

"So, go here. Pensacola Junior College. Didn't they give you a scholarship, too? You could keep your job at the bookstore, live here."

"There's nothing for me here!" Amanda cried out, exasperated.

"Why can't you be a normal kid? Make some real friends. Get a boyfriend. Hell, get laid, but stay here."

"I have friends."

"You have a couple of girls you hang out with when you aren't working. I think you'd rather be working, which is weird. You don't even understand how to have fun like a normal..."

Amanda cut her off. "I am going to NYU. That's where my scholarship is for," she flat-out lied, "and that is where I am going to attend."

Her mother's jaw snapped shut midsentence, and she glared at Amanda. Both of them hardened their stances. If either one had been capable of self-reflection in the moment, they would have realized they looked almost identical, green eyes flashing, locked in combat, jaws tight, arms crossed.

"You are an ungrateful little bitch, Amanda Melissa McDaniel. I am fucking done with you."

Caroline stormed out of the house. Amanda didn't even have it in her anymore to cry over it. She went to the kitchen, washed and put away her mother's dishes, and went to bed.

After that, Caroline didn't come back until the weekend. She stayed away from their apartment for days on end in the months that followed, coming home only to grab some clean clothes, which Amanda had washed, as always, before heading back out to whatever activities her social life held in store for her. Caroline even refused to attend Amanda's high school graduation in late May, which hurt Amanda more than she cared to admit. Meanwhile, Amanda was determined to spend her summer working as many hours as she could get, hanging out with friends – her real friends, going to the beach, and organizing her belongings so she could take everything with her. It was her plan to never come back to Florida if she could help it.

On a scorching July day, Amanda got a true taste of her future. An appetizer to tide her over until she left for New York the following month. She, Lisa, Pam, and Andrea wanted to go to the beach, but even the idea of the ocean couldn't lure them into the sun. They decided to stay inside at Lisa's house because her parents kept the air conditioning the coldest. While they sat around the living room and worked through a case of soda and a bag of chips they'd picked up on the way over, Lisa pulled out an old Ouija board that had belonged to her mother. She said her mother got it from her grandma, so this board was super old.

"No way," Pam declared, shaking her head. "I'm not screwing with demons or whatever. Those things are trouble."

"Seriously?" Lisa asked. She gently held the well-worn box with "Ouija" emblazoned across the middle in four-inch high block letters, "The Mystifying Oracle – Wonderful Talking Board" written in a smaller, more fanciful lettering below that. A mysterious blue-robed figure, with its face obscured by its own sleeve, gestured toward the player as if to say, "Learn my secrets, if you dare."

"Seriously. That's a gateway to demonic possession. It's a mortal sin or something. I'm Catholic." Pam kept her distance from the box with her hands outstretched as if to ward off evil.

"There's no such thing as demons or evil spirits or whatever," Amanda added, rolling her eyes. "It's just a game."

Andrea moved their chips off of the dining room table, and Lisa set the box down. "My mom says my grandma used to play this with her all the time. Grams was really good at getting answers. I did it with her a couple times. It was fun."

Pam maintained her skeptical look. Amanda went in for the kill.

"Don't you want to know if Mark Harter even knows you're alive?"

Pam looked swayed. She'd been secretly in love with the basketball player in their class since middle school. At least, she thought it was a secret. Seeing an opening, Lisa piled on.

"You go first!"

Pam conceded out of curiosity, and all four girls sat down at the table. They eagerly pulled the board from the box. It was the laminated Masonite version, and Amanda promptly scratched her hand on a sharp corner, leaving a red trail of raw skin near her wrist, just the faintest trace of blood. Andrea pulled out the creamed-colored plastic planchette with the little felt feet and held it until everyone was ready. Lisa, as the nominal owner of the game, sat in front of the board with all of the writing facing her. Andrea and Pam flanked her while Amanda sat at the top of the game, looking at the board upside down. Lisa instructed each of them to delicately place their fingers on the planchette, close their eyes and concentrate. They could look when the spirits started to answer.

"Okay, Pam. Go ahead and ask the great spirits your question," Lisa solemnly intoned.

"Oh, great spirits," Pam began, setting off a round of giggling at the table. "Stop it, you guys! Oh, great spirits," she began again, "Does Mark Harter love me?"

They collectively held their breath. Slowly, the planchette began to inch toward the "Yes" next to the smiling sun in the upper left-hand corner. As it grew closer and closer to Pam, she let out an involuntary squeal of delight. The planchette settled, its tear-dropped tip pointing directly at the affirmative answer. The girls took a short break to discuss Mark Harter's finer qualities: his dreamy eyes, his cool persona, his car. There was general agreement that Pam would have to make an excuse to see Mark at his job, so he could declare his love for her. There was also a lot more giggling.

"Me next, me next!" Andrea said. "Should I wait for Jesse when he goes away to college?"

The planchette scooted to "No" pretty fast, much to Andrea's dismay.

This provoked more in-depth discussion among the friends about the situation. It was only the University of Florida, so it wasn't so far, but Jesse was going into the dorms with some friends. He promised he would stay faithful to Andrea, but she was really waffling about just breaking up with him. She'd heard the horror stories of the high school girlfriend left behind. Besides, there was this other guy in her homeroom last year who was pretty cute. Maybe it was time to move on.

Lisa asked some general questions about her boyfriend, Robert. Amanda thought it sounded like she didn't trust him, so she deftly maneuvered the planchette to suggest that Lisa do some asking around. The yes and no answers hinted that the board was suspicious of Robert. Better safe than sorry if you were actually having sex with a person.

Amanda was having fun because she was the one driving the planchette. While keeping her eyes closed in a show of concentration, she was actually peeking out from beneath her lashes. Meanwhile, she was lightly guiding the planchette across the board to secure answers for her eager friends. She was trying to steer the questions to simple yes or no answers because she was finding it hard to spell anything while looking at the board upside down.

Finally, it was her turn to ask the board a question.

She opted for the same route her friends took.

"Oh, great spirits, will I find the love of my life at NYU?"

With her friends staring at the board in rapt attention, the planchette slid effortlessly to "Yes." For a second, she thought maybe one of the other girls was nudging it because it glided more easily this time, and she hadn't fully made up her mind about where she was going to place it.

There were oooohs and aaaahs all around. Then Pam blurted out, "What's his name?"

While Amanda was trying to decide what to name her prospective lover, the planchette jerked beneath her fingertips. She caught a faint whiff of a salty sea breeze and felt a slight tingle of electricity where her fingers met the planchette. Her eyes flew open in surprise.

"It's spelling something!"

Letters appeared in the window of the planchette in rapid-fire succession as it stuttered across the board, stopping only long enough for the girls to verbally register its choice from the alphabet.

"C... T... H... U..."

"That's not a name," Lisa protested.

"L... H... U..."

Amanda felt the give as whoever was driving the planchette let go of their control of it. She fell forward and had to release the planchette to catch herself. The scratch on her hand throbbed painfully, reminding her of her earlier injury. She looked suspiciously at her friends.

"What kind of name is that? I think your Ouija board is broken, Lisa."

"Yeah, 'Pat, I'd like to buy a vowel,'" Andrea said, snickering.

Mildly disappointed with their final interaction with the Ouija board and getting bored of gossiping in general, they put away the game and settled down to watch some TV with bowls of ice cream to beat the heat. But Amanda couldn't get over her unease at the revelations of the board. What was it trying to spell, really? And which one of her friends was pushing for that strange answer? Amanda may not have known the answers to those questions, but she did know one thing for certain.

She was never touching a Ouija board ever again.

And twenty years later, she still hadn't.

CHAPTER 3

I met Cthulhu when I was in college. I was young, naïve, and excited to be away from home, the place I'd considered a prison for most of my life.

He was one of those things.

We each needed a final General Education class in our senior year, and both of us chose Intro to Biology. We were assigned as each other's lab partners. We were dating by Week 3, and we slept together for the first time before midterms. It was a wild ride.

Until it wasn't.

And now, after everything that had happened, after everything I had learned about Ryley and about myself, here I was wandering through the city with him like it was old times. But it wasn't old times. It was here, and it was now, and nothing was the same, but I had to pretend because I had some unfinished business to resolve. His voice rumbling across my senses brought me out of my own head, a small mercy for which I was grateful.

"Is beer still a thing, Amanda? I enjoyed that quite a bit."

"Yeah, and you're really going to enjoy craft beer," I said, lightly stroking his arm as I held it. "It's big with the hipsters."

"Hipsters?"

"I'll explain as we walk."

By now, the crowd had reformed, and we were just two more tourists in the throng, strolling arm-in-arm, deciding on a place to get some grub while I explained the concept of hipsters to an alien god.

"So I would say, 'I liked craft beer before it was cool?'"

"Exactly," I replied with a chuckle.

"Well then, I did. I do remember beer. Cold and yeasty. Just not that over-hopped stuff."

Ryley pulled a face that indicated his opinion on hops – an Elder God brought low by a humble flower.

Yup. That was the charming Ry I remembered.

"My treat." He turned to a young man walking past us. "Give me your wallet."

The startled man looked at Ry. The man was dressed down, but it was an affected casual from a high-end store, most likely. He wore aviator sunglasses and a distressed brown light bomber jacket over a white t-shirt and jeans. As a writer, people watching was my stock in trade. This guy was "trust fund baby" right out of central casting, and he was about the same height and build as Ry.

I could tell the second their eyes connected. The man's jaw went completely slack, and he reached into his front pocket to retrieve the wallet. He'd probably put it there to ward off pick-pockets, but he was out of his league. He was lost.

"Don't, Ry. There's no need. I have plenty of…"

"Nonsense. I need a new start." Ry took the wallet and began to place it into his own back pocket.

Knowing I wouldn't win this particular argument, I tried to lessen the damage. "That guy will have to spend forever getting new credit cards and ID. Security has really gotten tight since you've been away. You don't need any of that stuff anyway, right?"

Ry looked at me with a cold stare. It was uncomfortable, but I held my ground.

"Always the do-gooder."

His mercurial mood was shifting, which wouldn't be good for anyone, least of all me. Ry didn't like being denied anything. He stood a moment, brooding over whether or not he wanted to do the right thing, the human thing. The thing I wanted him to do.

Finally, Ry sighed, removing the cash from the wallet. I saw several Benjamins as Ryley counted it before stuffing the wad into the front pocket of his jeans. It was a substantial amount, which both validated my original call that he was likely from money and lessened my sympathy for someone who was foolish enough to carry that much cash. Ryley handed the wallet back to the still stupefied man.

"Fine. But I want your jacket. It would look good on me. Give it to me. Now."

Unblinking, the man dropped his wallet to more expediently remove his jacket, handing it to Ryley, who immediately slipped it on. It fit like it was tailored. Still, the young man stood before us, stunned, unmoving.

I stooped down to retrieve his wallet from the ground. I tried handing it to the man, but he didn't even acknowledge my existence. Ry was his whole world now. There was nothing else left to him.

Sensing my frustration, Ryley stepped in again with more commands. "Take the wallet," Ry said, his anger simmering. "Put it away."

Like a computer program that needed every step coded to run, the man took the wallet from my hands and stuffed it into his back pocket.

"Excellent." Ry tugged the sleeves down to his wrists. "Give me your sunglasses."

Those were also handed over without question.

"Ray-Bans. Nice." His mood seemed to lift once again. "Go away now."

The man turned and stumbled back into the crowd of tourists. I had no idea how he would mentally justify giving his cash, sunglasses, and jacket to a stranger in New York City, but I knew it would happen. It always did. That was one of the small things that made Ryley so damn dangerous.

He put on the sunglasses. "Ah, that cuts the glare. The sun can be so nasty." Ryley put his hand out towards me, and I took it tentatively. "Let's go get that beer."

When we arrived at the little brewpub in Lower Manhattan, I suffered that familiar pang of guilt, knowing how Ryley would likely act. But I had a mission. I needed that favor, and I would do whatever it took to get my life back. Indulging Ryley's passions was a critical step in that direction.

"A 'flight' of beer is just a bunch of small ones for tasting? What a novel idea!" He turned to our server to make sure he caught her eyes. "Bring a flight for each of us and two each of your appetizers. Appetizers are still a 'thing,' aren't they?" he asked me as an aside.

I assured him they were as I watched the server's eyes glaze over, her whole being shifting to serve his whims.

"Two of each. And put our order first. We're the only table that matters to you."

She nodded silently and returned almost inhumanly fast with our beer.

"Keep 'em coming."

She nodded again and departed our table.

"You don't have to do that. The service here is pretty good as it is."

"I hate to wait. Especially for people," he said, breathing the last word with disgust. "You know, I'm thrilled you called me back to you. Disappointed you waited years but glad to be back Morningstar."

"It's great to see you again, too," I half-lied, trying to hide my involuntary flinching as he again used his pet name for me. "Now, about that favor…"

"More beer. Excellent!" He drained the remainder of his beer while the server stood waiting, holding the new flights. Because he was in a hurry to get his new beers, he drained mine as well. He pointed to the darkest beer in the bunch. "I want this one from now on. Just this one. Bring me pitchers and a larger glass. Now."

Again, wordlessly, the server set down the flights, cleared the empties from the table, and rushed off for more beer.

"College sure was instructional. If I'd have known about beer, I would have walked among people much sooner."

"Not like you had much of a choice."

"True, but majoring in Comparative Religion was a stroke of genius on my part. I learned about the competition and how to play beer pong. And do a keg stand! You remember that night?"

Of course, I did. His question was rhetorical. Having been a hard-studying wallflower for my first three years, Ryley had convinced me to attend a local frat party the Fall semester we met. We shotgunned beers and did keg stands. We played beer pong and quarter bounce until the wee hours. I got so wasted. I could hardly stand on my own two feet. Then one of the frat boys tried to entice me upstairs to his room. To relax. To get away from the crowd.

Ry stepped in, as calm as could be, and told him I was not available. He should go away.

Forever.

The following Monday, the student newspaper headlined the story about a frat brother who seemingly wandered away from a weekend party, walked a few blocks west through the Village, crossed the highway, and drowned in the Hudson River. His body was found the next day by a passing jogger in Hudson River Park.

That was my first and last college party.

My stomach clenched at the memories.

"Who could forget?" I tried to act nonchalant about it but downed one of the beers in my flight in a gulp.

"You were always so uptight in college. I am glad I could teach you to live a little."

"Unlike you, I had to work for my scholarships and for every good grade I pulled."

"I got good grades."

My laugh sounded more like a bark, which I saw did not go over particularly well. "You mesmerized the professors! You never had to crack a book if you didn't want to. I don't even know if you took classes before we met."

He made a scoffing noise.

"Hell, Ry, you didn't even have an education when you came to the university. You made the counselors admit you and schedule your classes. You persuaded them to give you full scholarships. You never had to work for anything at school."

"I worked for you."

"Did you? I always wondered how many of my feelings were your suggestions." I had to force myself to consciously stop twisting my hands in my lap. Old insecurities die hard.

"I needed you to love me. And you did. That was real." His voice was soft and low, setting off just the right thrum in my chest.

"Was it? I don't think I'll ever know."

"It was real. I couldn't make you help me. You had to do that of your own accord."

He accepted another pitcher of beer from our server. Then she brought enough appetizers that she had to pull up a second table to hold it all. When a few other patrons gave us a dirty look, Ryley caught their eyes and stared hard. Most of them immediately threw money onto their tables and left. One guy at the bar choked on his beer and passed out on the floor. The server merely stepped around him.

"Speaking of helping you, how is your 'family' doing?"

"Don't call them that," Ryley snapped.

"You used to."

"Well, they're not. They're fucking stupid cultists. I hope they're all dead." Ryley's eyes turned cold, and he slammed his glass down on the table with such ferocity that a few of the remaining patrons visibly jumped in their seats.

"I can assure you that at least some of them are alive and kicking," I said, taking a sip of my beer. "They sometimes turn up at my book signings. I've had to hire security for each event."

"Perhaps now that I'm back, I can make sure they don't bother you, or anyone else, ever again." He drained the last of the pitcher into his own glass.

"Which is why I wanted to talk to you…"

"More beer!" he shouted to our server. "And more of these…" He lowered his voice for me, "What do you call these things?"

"Devils on Horseback."

"They're delicious." He resumed his yelling for our server. "And several orders of Devils on Horseback. I want all of them."

She disappeared into the kitchen.

"What were those things you used to make for me that I liked? White and yellow. Soft. Devil's something or other."

"Deviled eggs?"

"Yes, those! They were wonderful."

He yelled to no one in particular, "I want deviled eggs!"

Alarmingly, his power to influence seemed to have increased since his return. I suspected that it was his proximity to my little nautilus and its harnessed power. His corrupting influence seemed to permeate the entire establishment. The kitchen staff was likely enthralled. Our server would need therapy if she hovered around our table too much longer. What should have been a busy late weekday in a happening Manhattan hotspot had turned sour. People finished their food and left in silence. No one remained at the bar. No people came in, despite the Trip Advisor recommendations and picture-perfect posts from dozens of Instagram influencers. We were the sole focus of the entire establishment, as Ryley commanded it to be.

"Why do people name their food after the things they fear? I think the allure of the Devil is too much for you to resist." He smiled at me, and my stomach fluttered a little in spite of knowing what I knew. He was right.

Evil did have some sex appeal.

I could only imagine the frenzy in the kitchen that resulted in Devils on Horseback and deviled eggs appearing in quantity at our table just a few minutes later. Ryley tucked in with gusto, devouring everything on the table and swigging several pitchers of beer to wash it down.

When you had the metabolism of a god, you could get away with a lot of overeating. I'd always been a bit jealous of that. Maybe even more than just a bit.

"Can we please talk about my favor now?"

He pouted. "If you must. I was really just trying to enjoy my first good meal in fifteen years. In fact, I'm done. Let's go for a walk."

I sighed. There was no use in pushing him. Ryley only did things in his own time.

He stood abruptly and walked over to the still unconscious patron on the floor. Ryley kicked him hard and barked his orders. "Wake up! You need to carry our bag."

The man snapped alert and scrambled to get my weekend luggage. I didn't bother to fight. This was going to be how it was going to be.

I got up, knowing Ryley had no intention of paying for anything. He never did. For him, dine-n-dash was a mind-bending art form. I thought about sneaking a few twenty-dollar bills under my plate for the staff when they shook off their stupor, but it didn't come close to covering the damage Ryley left in his wake. I decided against it.

We headed out into the early evening.

Ryley hailed a cab and had us taken to Times Square, including the hapless bar patron who was now our porter. We strolled in silence for a while as Ryley took in the sights and sounds like any New York City tourist. He reveled in the crowded commotion here. We wandered down to Rockefeller Center, where his only comment was that he remembered a large tree being there before. He liked it better with the ice.

Bored with walking around, he flagged down another taxi cab and had us taken to Central Park. He seemed to enjoy walking around in the park, although he spooked all of the horses pulling carriages. He could bend the carriage drivers to his will, but the horses knew better. They instinctively knew what he was and wouldn't settle enough for us to get anywhere near them, let alone take a ride.

When he tired of seeing the old sights, he made a beeline to the most luxurious hotel in the city, a stately property known for its Park views. Although after 15 years in the business, I made a good living as a writer, even I wouldn't be willing to pay what they asked for a night. It was out of my league. Suites here cost more per night than most of the cars I had ever owned.

To Ryley, however, that made it all the more desirable.

We walked up to the desk, and he waved away our impromptu porter, sending the poor man disoriented and dazed back out onto Fifth Avenue.

Within a few minutes, we were being escorted to a private waiting area in the lobby while they prepared our suite. I don't know if we displaced a celebrity or some member of a royal family, but half of the entourage was buzzing around the lobby like a swarm of angry wasps. For Ryley, this chaos was a feature, not a bug.

A bellhop soon arrived at our area to lead us up to our suite. He hadn't been commanded to do so because he didn't need to be to execute his job flawlessly. It was only the unfortunate clerks at the front desk who suffered this evening. Although the longer we stayed, the more his presence would poison the hotel.

We took a semi-private elevator to one of the top floors, and our bellhop let us into the nicest hotel room I'd ever seen. Immaculately spotless, it had three bedrooms, including a master bedroom with a terrace overlooking Central Park. A butler, in full formal butler's attire, stood waiting for us when we entered. Again, she was a professional and needed no magical influence to perform impeccably. We were her guests, and she would take care of all of our needs.

Ryley left explicit instructions with the butler regarding our evening. He told her he would be leaving his clothes outside the door to be cleaned and returned to him. He told her we were not to be disturbed under any circumstances. Finally, Ryley exclaimed he was "famished" and ordered enough dinner for a dozen people. There was no menu involved; he just rattled off a few of his favorites from his last visit to the city, including items from several prominent local restaurants. He also specifically requested Devils on Horseback and deviled eggs. And some decent wine. And a dessert. Something decadent. Maybe two. Our butler didn't bat an eye. She said, "Very good, sir," bowed slightly and left.

"Even for you, isn't this a little much?"

"Hey, if we're going to be reunited in New York City, we should enjoy it."

I noticed he said "we," and I sensed my chance.

"So, about my favor? I was hoping that you could…"

He took my hand and pulled me into the master bedroom, to the French doors just beyond the bed. He opened the doors, throwing them wide.

"With these views, Morningstar?"

Ryley steered me out onto the terrace and, I hated to admit, the view was incredibly distracting.

We stood on the terrace for a long while, me against the railing, and Ryley behind me, encircling me with both of his arms. I could feel his warm exhalations on my neck, his breathing even and slow, like waves lapping along a beach. Even though we were nowhere near the ocean, I could smell the faint but crisp redolence of the seas emanating from the man I'd loved all these years. It was a comfort and triggered warm memories. As we watched a sensational sunset over the city skyline, I reveled in the lie of his humanity and the feel of my lover's arms around me after so many years away. I hadn't been with anyone before Ryley or since. It had been a desolate stretch of my life, empty even with the fame and success, and I still didn't know if the feeling of belonging and coming home to someone was real.

I suspected it wasn't.

As the sun set, the night sky darkened as much as it could for the city that never sleeps. Above us, the new constellation came into view. Nicknamed Trekkie by the media, due to its similarity to the Starfleet insignia from the Star Trek franchise, this new and vibrant constellation was best viewed from the Northeastern Coast of the United States. I was betting I knew the exact location of the prime viewing spot: an old, rundown house on a nondescript spit of land jutting out from the shore at the edge of Highlands in New Jersey. That's where Ryley's "family" had a compound riddled with insanity and brimming with deranged cultists. The place where he was born into this world almost twenty years ago.

The light from the stars shifted colors every night, growing brighter every few weeks. This had been the talk of astronomers and other scientists for months, ever since it began winking into existence late last year, one star at a time. City dwellers were enamored of it because it was the only constellation they could see in the night sky unless there was a citywide blackout. The constellation was especially intriguing and unfathomable to the scientists because it was only bright enough to view in the evenings over the East Coast, never in other parts of the world. It was an impossibility that confounded astronomy experts, but I and a very few select others knew the truth. Not only did the light from these stars not come from within our galaxy cluster, but it was possible it didn't even come from our universe or our reality.

Those weren't ordinary stars, and this wasn't natural science in play. Dark forces worked to create Trekkie, and the stars were aligning for a specific purpose. The light from a few more stars would become visible tonight, revealing Trekkie to look a whole lot more like the sigil I chalked onto the docks earlier today; although, most people watching the constellation would not know that. They would only keep that formation for a day or two more at most; then they would disappear even more suddenly than they appeared.

Which was why I chose this exact time to call Ryley.

"You know what I have missed the most about New York City?" Ry whispered in my ear.

"Mmmm?"

"You."

I turned to face him. I could see him clearly in the soft glow of the city's lights, even after sunset. He appeared so sincere, looking at me with a slight tilt to his head. I could never know whether or not to believe his words, but his expression was another story.

Impulsively, I kissed him.

I ran my fingers into his thick hair and pulled him as close to me as I could get, devouring him. He tasted like a maelstrom racing across the seas, rocking me like a boat tossed about in the waves.

He reciprocated, pulling my hips tight into his, grinding his body against me.

Kissing Ryley and listening to the sounds of the city drifting up from below pulled me back through time until I was just a naïve young woman finishing college with her first boyfriend, the love of her life. I wanted to be that girl again, if only for a few moments. I felt I deserved that, at least.

Ryley intensified the kiss, and my body thrummed to his call. He picked me up, his mouth still locked onto mine, and carried me back inside.

He set me down on my feet next to the bed. We undressed each other with great haste. He savagely ripped the duvet from the bed, tossing it aside, and pushed me backward, riding me down onto the sheets.

His hands roamed across my body. I gave as good as I got, feeling the curve of his neck and digging my nails into the muscles of his shoulders. Wantonly, I dragged my nails across his back, hard enough to draw blood, I was sure, and he groaned in response.

Ryley and I both enjoyed it a little rough.

We nipped and bit at each other's necks, although he was careful never to touch my pendant or its silver chain. Our hands roamed lower on our bodies, becoming ever more insistent. I broke it off first, twisting out from under him, so I could lay beside him, still running my hands feverishly across his body.

It should have felt odd for me, lying with the same man after all these years. Especially odd since he was still in the prime of his youth physically, while I had aged into my late thirties. Instead, I felt young again, energized. And Ryley didn't seem to notice our age difference at all. This proved just a momentary distraction before I lost myself again in the sensations of our bodies coming together.

Our lovemaking was wild and urgent, both of us sensing that our time together was precious. Our foreplay, in the past lasting hours as we enjoyed the feel of each other, was kept minimal and intense.

He allowed me to rub him and touch him and arouse him to the brink, then he rolled back on top of me and kissed his way down my body. I arched into him, feeling my core tighten like an overwound spring. My orgasm rocked me so hard that I screamed out. He stayed down for just a moment more to torment me, then aggressively crawled up my body and entered me fully.

I clung to the bedsheets, digging in for purchase, and Ryley rode me as hard as he ever had. When he came, I did again, too. We were growling and roaring like animals until Ryley rolled off, head crashing into the pillows.

We both lay there panting, trying to catch our breath until Ryley rolled over to grab the pile of bedding from the floor. He managed to throw it over both of us, shielding us from the chill night air coming in from the still ajar French doors.

He'd always been considerate like that.

He wedged his left arm beneath me to pull me close to his still sweaty chest, pulled the duvet up to nearly our chins. He lightly kissed my head, and we both dropped off to sleep.

I don't know when exactly I woke up, but the glow from the city was still pouring in through the French doors. So was the cold. I got up from the bed and closed them, looking back at Ryley still sleeping.

He looked every inch the god he was, albeit in human form. He was tangled in the sheets, but I saw one muscular thigh peeking out from the white cotton. He had one arm thrown over his head, which was turned slightly to the side. His dark curls cascaded across his pillow, and his lips were parted ever so slightly as he breathed deep and even. His olive complexion was pretty uniform all over his body without the variations one would normally see from a person who wore clothes and spent time outdoors. He never had any tan lines, and his skin tone was a single shade over his entire body. That was one of the things that I noticed when we first got together, when we first became lovers. Although there was no way I could have possibly fathomed why that was. Even now, I found it disconcerting because it was so unnatural, especially as my own belly was a very unflattering shade of pale even compared to my own arms.

There was the faint smell of petrichor in the room, like after a summer storm. Ryley brought the wildness of the oceans and the storms and the winds wherever he went. It was a huge part of my attraction to him from the very beginning. And some things didn't change.

I tiptoed around the bedroom, grabbing a hotel bathrobe from a hook behind the door. It was perhaps the softest, fluffiest robe I had ever experienced. I immediately considered stealing it, but then the pang of guilt hit. Of course, wasn't I, in fact, stealing the whole suite as it was? Didn't that make stealing the robe kind of a gimme, in terms of ethics, or at least in terms of value? Maybe I'd stuff it into my luggage after all.

That would be a problem for later in the day. Maybe even tomorrow.

Shaking off the feeling, I tied the sash and went to the suite's dining room. All of the food Ryley ordered earlier was on the table covered by ornamental silver cloches. The table itself was set with platinum-rimmed china, Waterford crystal, and polished silver. There was a chocolate fondue kept warm by a small burner, rimmed with cake – Angel food cake, I discovered, as I popped a piece in my mouth. There was also a cake that would have been at home in a moderately-priced wedding, with three layers, frosting, and minimal decoration beyond a few rosettes. Lifting many of the cloches to browse, I picked a couple of pieces of wine-poached lobster from one and a few slices of NYC deli pastrami with an authentic half-sour pickle from another. I poured myself a goblet of the Syrah that had been opened and left in a chiller that kept it at the perfect 64 degrees.

I set my feast at a seat facing another terrace where I could see the city lights spread out below me. I could see the lights in Central Park and imagine a carriage ride there.

I pulled my feet up onto the dining room chair, snuggled into my robe, and looked out onto the tableau. "Here's to life, for however long it lasts," I said, toasting to an empty room.

"It can last forever," Ryley interrupted, startling me. He was standing at the opposite end of the table, wearing the other hotel robe from our bedroom. His dark curls could best be described as tousled in that "just had wild sex" look I adored seeing on him.

Because I knew that sex was with me.

"I didn't mean to wake you," I stammered.

He smiled and tilted his head. "You making a joke, Morn-ingstar?"

When I realized what I'd said, I flushed a deep, mortified red.

"No, I didn't mean this afternoon. I just meant that…" I trailed off, scrunching up my nose in an act of embarrassment. Then the reality of our situation slammed back into me full force. If I lived beyond the next few days, I knew my gaffe would haunt me.

He laughed and waved away my discomfort. "Too bad. It would have been a good joke."

He walked over, kissed the top of my head, then picked up a plate and piled it high with the hotel's offerings, except for the lobster. Ryley never ate seafood. He sat his plate down in front of the chair directly next to me, then, as an afterthought, brought the entire platter of deviled eggs over and placed it next to his plate. He gestured for his own goblet, and I obliged, pouring for him. He tucked into the upscale fare like a man on a mission.

"I've really missed take out," he said, as he polished off most of a Peking duck with the accompanying scallion pancakes.

"Me, too," I said wistfully, managing to get one nice bite of the crispy skin from the duck before it was gone.

"You could order take out anytime," Ryley said, finally

slowing down after demolishing most of the spread, including a good chunk of the cake.

"Not up in Connecticut, I mean, not like this. Well, we actually have white clam pizza, and that's pretty damn good."

"I thought you said seafood didn't belong on pizza?"

"Connecticut proved me wrong, but I usually ordered and picked up instead of getting delivery. Couldn't be too careful about giving out my address to delivery drivers," I said.

"It's hard being a single woman living alone. At least that's what you used to tell me about your mom."

"That too, but especially not with your family members on the prowl."

"Stop calling them that. They're no family of mine."

"Okay, not with *cultists* looking for me." I split the last of our bottle of Syrah between us and went for the second bottle of wine. It was definitely going to be a two bottle kind of night. Maybe three… maybe more.

"And now that you're back, you've lit up their Ouija boards and their crystal balls like a goddamn beacon. We probably don't have much time." I polished off my goblet and poured myself another, taking a hearty sip.

He actually looked concerned. "Did they hurt you? When I was gone?"

I thought back to that night, the night Ryley went back to the ocean. "I mean, yeah, that night, but I got away."

"You were supposed to be with me. I could have protected you. How did we get separated? I don't remember anything after we touched the gate. Next thing I knew, I was dreaming of you but not with you."

I looked briefly into his eyes, trying to ascertain whether or not that was the truth. He was hard to read, and I was out of practice. Still unsure, I gazed into my wine, a lovely, smooth Pinot Noir. What a contrast to the chaos of that last night with Ryley. How could I tell him about what I saw, the horror of his true form? How could I tell him how it broke me? How could I explain to him that he was the nightmare that fueled my research and my writing career? If not for the immediate pain of a cultist's knife in my side, I might never have gotten free that night, physically or mentally.

CHAPTER 4

Fifteen Years Ago

The sleek, silver BMW Z8 coasted to a silent stop, one of the many benefits of a manual transmission. The overgrown half-moon driveway of the dilapidated Victorian mansion looked like something from a black and white movie, bleached of color by the light of a full moon. The house itself, teetering on the edge of a bluff, overlooked the ocean. From the passenger seat, Amanda could see moonlight reflecting off the distant water through the tangled, leafless limbs of the few trees around the house.

"No place like home," Ryley said, setting the parking brake.

Amanda looked over at Ryley as he considered the place he'd left a few years ago. He looked stunning as ever with his light green Oxford shirt, unbuttoned to show the top of his chest. His dark curls brushed his collarbone as always, but the signature twinkle in his eyes was gone. He was clearly agitated about being here again.

"This is it," she said, trying to hide her disappointment.

"This is it," he echoed.

After cruising by the multi-million dollar homes along the route, Amanda wasn't sure what she had been expecting, but it certainly wasn't this. Whereas all of the other houses within miles of here were lit up with security lights and tucked away behind tastefully painted cement walls lined with cameras and 'No Trespassing' signs, Ryley's family lived on a property that was surrounded by an ancient-looking gothic iron fence. There wasn't even a gate across the front. They'd just driven right up to the creepy-looking front door unchallenged.

"You sure no one's here?" Amanda asked apprehensively, peering out her window.

"Positive. I told you, everyone is at a big, important family celebration tonight. It's like a ritual. We'll have the place all to ourselves."

Ryley got out, walked around the car, and opened Amanda's door for her. She was unused to riding in such a nice car. Having any car in New York City was a serious luxury, but Ryley had insisted that there was no other way to access his house. As it was a stealth mission, he certainly couldn't ask anyone in his family for a ride, he'd reasoned. Luckily, a friend of his let him borrow the car for the evening. He helped her up from the low leather seat, then he reached into the backseat and pulled out a metal flashlight that could double as a formidable club. He closed the door, leaving the car unlocked. He held the flashlight in his right hand and took Amanda's hand with his left.

"If no one is home, how are you going to find your passport? For that matter, how are we even going to get into the house?" she asked as they stepped onto the creaky front porch. She held Ryley's hand tightly as the rickety boards groaned and pitched beneath her feet. The whole porch looked like it was going to slump to the ground. He helped her to the threshold.

"We're going to get in because they always," Ryley let go of Amanda and stretched to reach above the door frame, pulling down an old-fashioned skeleton key, "keep a spare nearby." He wiggled his eyebrows and smiled warmly at Amanda, making her giggle. Turning to the door, he inserted the key and turned it. The sound of the door latch unlocking reverberated like a gunshot in the still night. Amanda jumped.

"Don't be so nervous. There's nothing here to worry about. Nothing I can't handle." He put the spare key back on its perch, threw open the door, stepped inside, and turned to offer her his hand. "Welcome to Novastella Manor, m'lady." He bowed slightly.

She followed him inside.

Even with the strong beam of the flashlight, the house seemed extraordinarily dark to Amanda. It was like it was somehow absorbing the light. She tried to shake the eerie feeling that had plagued her since they pulled up a few minutes ago. After all, it was Ryley's ancestral home. How bad could it be?

Pretty bad, she discovered.

Amanda was a little dismayed that the inside was as shabby and deteriorated as the outside. Since Ryley always had the best of everything, she assumed he came from money. Not that she had much of a frame of reference on good living, coming from her background as a former trailer park dweller from Tallahassee, but she certainly hadn't expected that Ryley's family lived in such an old, ramshackle house. Any family that would hold their son's passport to keep him from traveling might be eccentric, but she thought they would also have the means to travel and thus the means to maintain a very nice house. On the Jersey Shore, no less!

If Ryley noticed that Amanda was put off by the house, he didn't show it. Instead, he took her hand and made his way steadily toward the back of the house. The hallway kept turning at 90-degree angles, zigzagging through the house like a maze. She was already not sure she could find her way back out. It was the strangest layout she'd ever seen.

"Do you have any idea where they might have hidden your passport? It seems like a lot of rooms. It could be any of them."

"I have a pretty good idea where to find it, but there's something else I want to show you first. The view of the ocean from the beach is unlike any other. You'll love it."

Amanda was only catching brief glimpses of rooms before they passed them. They finally reached a long hallway that seemed to stretch out forever. She'd never seen an architectural layout like this before. She wasn't even sure how all of this fit within the footprint of the house. Many of the doors along the way were closed, but the open rooms seemed to have an abundance of chairs and strange paintings. It looked to her like an endless array of meeting rooms, more like a conference center than a home.

"Are we going to go upstairs and see your room? We could, you know, do it on your old bed or something." She tried to laugh, but it sounded forced, even to her own ears. This house was making her increasingly uncomfortable.

"My room isn't upstairs. I have something way better in mind."

They finally passed by a dining room so large, it could have served as a banquet hall. The dining room table looked like it might seat a few dozen people. She actually pulled Ryley to a halt to take a second look. More grotesque paintings lined the walls, covering almost every inch, jammed nearly frame to frame. The chair at the head of the table could only be described as a throne. It was made of heavy, dark wood and displayed the oddest carvings. The ceiling had been painted to resemble the night sky, but all of the constellations looked out of place or distorted. Actual gas globes flickered in sconces around the room.

"This is weird," Amanda said, entering the room to examine the chair closely. "There are these strange sea monster things carved into it. What is that about? And who still has their house on gas? Don't you have electricity?"

"My family has a fetish for folklore about the sea. I told you, they're not like everyone else. And, no, they never upgraded to electricity. C'mon. We're wasting time." Ryley grabbed her hand a little more forcefully than was strictly necessary and restarted his trek to the back of the house.

"You sure there's no one here? There could be a dozen people running around, and it would be hard to tell. This place is huge."

"Positive."

Ryley traipsed through the kitchen, which appeared industrial in design and capacity. Amanda marveled at the extra stoves, which looked like the wood burners from the old days. None of the appliances looked new or even modern. There appeared to be an honest-to-goodness icebox in the corner. Multiple kitchen islands filled the space, one topped with what appeared to be white marble glowed in the moonlight pouring in through the floor-to-ceiling windows facing the ocean, the rest of darker material. Heavy oak cupboards lined an interior wall in the cavernous space. There were even two large stone fireplaces on an outside wall, each looking big enough to stand in, and one of them with an enormous copper pot sitting in the hearth.

"Who even cooks like this anymore? Whoa!" Amanda wanted to linger to have a look at the old school kitchen, but Ryley pulled her ever toward the back, only stopping at a counter long enough to turn off and set down the flashlight. Now, with the expansive kitchen windows and nearing the outside, they didn't really need extra light. Moonlight flooded in the windows, bathing the whole kitchen in its harsh, cold glare.

Leaving her question unanswered, they finally got to the back door. Ryley opened it, and they both stepped out into the backyard.

Amanda's nostrils were assailed by the scent of the ocean,

tinged with an undercurrent of some unpleasant and unidentifiable stench like something had died nearby. It was just enough to be noticeable but not quite enough to ruin the gorgeous view.

The house was perched on a bluff, overlooking a deserted expanse of beach. In the backyard itself, statuary littered the landscape, although there appeared to be only one path toward the water. The rest of the yard looked unkempt and overgrown. As Amanda and Ryley walked the path, they passed ornate water fountains with pools of dark water in the bottom. Amanda suspected that might be where the off smell was coming from. She attributed a light breeze to her outbreak of goosebumps as they passed a particularly surreal statue of an octopus-headed man.

"Your family is really into art," she said, wrinkling her nose a little at the horrible statues.

"Mmmm.."

She took his sound for agreement. Their path was illuminated by moonlight so bright, it was almost like daylight.

As they reached the edge of the bluff, Amanda could see a rickety staircase twisting its way down to the sand. The wood she could see looked weathered and splintered. It didn't look safe at all.

As Ryley started toward the stairs, Amanda hesitated, pulling back from him for the first time in their strange journey through the house and yard. She had assumed that he was just overwhelmed by being back at his family home, but she was getting a prickly feeling in the back of her neck, which had always reliably told her when something was wrong.

"Do we have to go down? I mean, those stairs, they aren't in the best of shape," she said, trying to reason with her suddenly distant boyfriend.

Apparently sensing her change in mood, Ryley stopped. Amanda could see him visibly attempt to soften his stance and demeanor, as he sometimes did when he was distracted and trying to come back into the conversation. He took both of her hands in his and looked at her, cocking his head slightly to one side.

"Don't you want to see the ocean?"

"I can see it from here. Can't we just enjoy the view from here? Then we can find your passport and get home to the city."

He gently turned her toward the ocean, standing behind her and pointing down to the shore. "See that arch down there?"

"Yeah."

"You have to see the way it frames the ocean. It will give you a perspective on the sea that you never even dreamed possible. I want to show it to you, Morningstar. More than anything, I want to share it with you." His last words were practically breathed into her right ear, and he ended by nuzzling her neck.

She knew she was lost.

"I just don't want to break my neck on those stairs."

"I'll lead the way. You can use my shoulders to hold for balance. I won't let anything or anyone ever hurt you. I promise."

They began their descent, slowly until Amanda got the hang of the sway of the steps and the railing, then a little quicker. After what seemed like an eternity to Amanda, she finally felt the relief of the sand beneath her shoes. As a Florida girl, she knew how to walk on sand, and that particular balancing act was a comfort to her.

One of the first things she noticed as they crossed the beach was that there weren't a lot of tracks. Most beaches were torn up by the tires of ATVs and the tread of the soles of hundreds, if not thousands, of tourists.

This sand looked pristine.

Even if the tide washed the sand smooth twice a day, beach-goers usually desecrated it almost immediately. It was the natural order of beach living, even on "private" beaches.

"How does your family keep everyone off their beachfront?

Lawyers? Electrified fence somewhere down the beach? I've never seen a beach so immaculate."

"No one comes to our beach. The family has owned this land for generations. It's always just been understood that outsiders are not welcome."

Amanda stopped walking at that, bringing Ryley to a halt with her.

"Don't worry. You're no outsider. You're mine." He smiled in that slightly predatory way that sometimes made Amanda feel sexy and wanted. And sometimes, it made her uncomfortable.

This was one of those times. The latter.

He overcame her inertia with a cajoling tug, and they covered the many yards from the stairs to the arch. She just wanted to see this spectacular view, get Ryley's passport, and then get the hell out of here.

From the bluff, the arch had looked like it was built from dark wood or something, but now, up close, Amanda could see it was made of some sort of stone. The distance from the bluff was also deceptive in showing the apparent size of the arch. It had seemed somehow…normal? from above. Even from the distance of the stairs, the arch had seemed to be just an arch on the beach, an odd architectural feature, but of normal-seeming size and shape.

Up close, however, Amanda thought the arch looked huge and imposing. The stones looked like something out of Stone-henge, unwieldy building blocks stacked uncertainly by an over-sized child. The two side pieces were of slightly different heights but well over her head. The crosspiece seemed precariously balanced upon them, leaning slightly back toward shore as if to crush a person unwary enough to be caught beneath it. Although the stones were huge, the space between them looking out to sea was only a few feet across like a standard doorway. It was misshapen and foreboding.

"You like it?" Riley asked, breaking Amanda's dark musings.

A chill ran through her, popping goosebumps on her arms.

"Not really, Ryley. What the hell is this thing?"

She balked at getting closer, then felt the insistent pressure of Ryley's hand at the small of her back.

"My family had it raised from a maritime site off the coast. Some ancient artifact. Like Stonehenge. Pretty cool, huh?" He again pushed her forward. "Wait until you see the view through it."

Finally, Amanda was standing before it. She now saw that the rounded edges she'd assumed were an archway was more squared off. It looked like dark green obsidian or black marble. Carved runes covered the stone as if a mad graffiti artist had tagged it. Some of the runes even appeared to move, which must have been a trick of the moonlight.

Amanda felt like she must be shaking pretty hard because her pendant, the cute little nautilus shell Ryley had given her, was quaking against her skin.

"Go on, Morningstar. Look through it."

"I don't want to."

"Look!" He pushed her forward, and she caught herself, one palm of each hand bracing against the miscreation.

In contrast to the suddenly cold night, the stones were warm beneath her touch. Her hands felt like they were melting into the stone.

Suddenly, she was looking into a dark mirror. She could see herself imposed faintly over the sea beyond. A bright light emanated from her chest. She looked closer and saw it was her pendant, glowing like a sun. The ocean kicked up, waves rising, jets of water shooting toward the sky. The sea roiled like it was boiling, fish rolling helplessly in the froth. She couldn't be sure if she saw the ocean through the opening or if she saw some odd reflection because it didn't seem real.

Then she used the reflection to look behind her.

There, instead of Ryley, stood the octopus-headed man from

the statue. Its hideous facial tentacles reaching toward her, toward the sea.

A whooshing sound assailed her, but the winds came from behind, buffeting her as they rushed past and into the reflection.

"Ryley, what's happening?" she screamed above the maelstrom. "What is this thing?"

He leaned forward, slamming his hands over hers, driving her palms further into the stone.

Even through the raging winds, she felt the soft tickle of his breath in her ear, as she had so many times before as his lover.

"This is our passport," he whispered.

In the reflection, it wasn't his breath that tickled her ear but the gentle brush of tentacles as they reached for the gate. Not being able to cope with these contradictions, Amanda blanked, her mind trying desperately to shield her from what could not be but clearly was.

Raw power continued to surge into the nautilus. The brightness emanating from the disjointed shell would have blinded Amanda if her eyes were still registering anything within this dimension.

Ryley, concentrating on the power transfer, did not notice his family arrive. It was the impact of one of the cult members tackling him, forcing him to release his grasp on Amanda's hands, that made him realize their dire change of circumstance.

As soon as Ryley's hands broke contact with Amanda, the power within the gate released itself into the necklace around Amanda's neck with unchecked ferocity. The resulting explosion blew Amanda off of the gate and onto the sand of the beach. The intensity of the light rushing from the gate was physical, something beyond the physics of this world. She watched as the last of the light fell away from the gate and shattered on the ground. Shards of light jutted up from the sand before seeming to melt into it. The light was concentrated and dazzling. The following day, newspapers would make note of the flash, which was reported as far away as Eastern Long Island. The media conjectured it was a meteor or other natural phenomenon. Conspiracy nuts had theories on everything from small nuclear explosions to crashed alien spaceships.

No one could even guess the truth.

Wind and water jetted out of the gate across the beach to the cliff face causing everyone there to be blown off their feet. Ryley and his assailant, already on the ground, were spared the brunt of the blast.

The beach buzzed with chaos. Ryley and the cultist were wrestling to gain control over each other. Amanda, staggering to regain her feet, gazed confused at the scene before her. People scrambled around while a short, skinny man shouted orders, trying to regain some form of order within the bedlam occurring around him.

Light still shone brightly from the nautilus around Amanda's neck, drawing the attention of the person trying to give orders. Like a moth to a flame, the leader was drawn to the power held within the shell. He started to cross the beach toward Amanda when the second wave struck the beach.

What started as a slight breeze funneled toward the gaping mouth of the gate turned violently into hurricane-force winds drawing everything in its path toward an unknowing future. The few cultists that had already regained their composure, and were moving in to subdue Ryley, were the first to be sucked through the gate. As each entered the threshold, an audible and wet popping sound announced their absence from the beach, akin to the sound of a breaking joint when parting out a chicken for supper. Although no one stopped to take notice during the melee, the survivors would find their sleep haunted with that sound for the remainder of their days.

Amanda, being on the edge of the reverse cannon blast, stood witness as Ryley and his assailant, still brawling in the sand, were slowly drawn toward the portal. Their bodies dug trenches in the sand as they were pulled across the beach. The force upon the two bodies increased as they grew nearer, finally dislodging them from each other. The pull of the gate forcibly evicted the cultist from the fight and flung him through the gate with that sickening telltale pop. No longer burdened by his foe, Ryley scrabbled to gain purchase on this side of reality. Twisting to his side, he managed to grab the edge of the gate, desperately trying to halt his ejection from this plane of existence. In his battle with the unnatural force of the maelstrom, Ryley locked eyes with Amanda.

"Morningstar!" he screamed, just as he lost his grip and plummeted into the abyss.

Amanda was raptly focused on Ryley's struggle, her muscles, and bones locked in place with her terror, keeping her from either assisting him or hindering him. When she heard the pop, everything went quiet. The pull, the storm, the winds – all of it followed Ryley through, leaving the gate inert, just a non-descript stack of rocks on the beach.

She heard a man scream out, "Stupid bitch! This is your fault!"

She barely registered him running up the beach towards her, so broken was her mind after all that had just transpired. Amanda felt like what came next happened in slow motion. She half-turned toward the leader of the cult, vaguely aware that the violent turmoil of the vortex had stopped. The man's dark hair was disheveled and wet, as if he had just stepped out of a riptide. He was wearing a red robe, which was also wet and caked in places with sand. The robe seemed to drag at him as he walked, leaving his gait burdened and uneven. She barely caught the flash of something silver in his hand, just as she felt a searing pain in her lower right back next to her kidney.

As she turned to face him, he was holding a bloody knife of some sort in his right hand.

She gasped. As their eyes connected, a look of recognition

crossed his face, and he dropped the blade onto the sand. His face went from purple with rage to ashen with fear in a moment.

"It...it's you!" he stammered. "The Morning Star. I didn't know. Forgive me!"

Amanda took this lapse in his assault to turn and make a run from the nightmare in which she found herself. She didn't know where she was going, but her mind finally registered enough of the madness to urge her to flee. In a blind panic, she pounded across the sand like her life depended upon it.

The pendant was still glowing, and its light intensified as the pain from being stabbed threatened to make her knees buckle. Still, she ran for the stairs leading back to the mansion. For a moment, the staircase, dozens of stairs twisting back and forth on themselves as they climbed into the darkness, seemed insurmountable. Then she heard her attacker yelling for her to wait, and she redoubled her efforts. The brighter the amulet shone, the easier her labored breathing became, allowing her to ascend the staircase in record time.

Amanda raced through the grotesque statuary, only flinching as she passed the particularly hideous octopus-man creature, now recognizing it as Ryley in his other form. Not bothering to check behind her for signs of pursuit, she opened the kitchen door, sprinting through, pulling it closed behind her. For the first time, she took a moment to catch her breath. She didn't see anyone coming up the path, but she knew she couldn't have more than a minute on her pursuer, at most. She stopped at the counter to grab the flashlight Ryley had used to guide them through the house, noticing for the first time that the lights were turned up. Holding the flashlight close to her chest, Amanda tried to calm her breathing, so she could listen for any movement from within the house. All she could hear was her own heartbeat pounding in her ears. In the flickering glow of the gas lamps, the kitchen looked more like a meat processing plant than a home kitchen, noticeable even in a home as strange as this one. Despite her shocked state, she now noticed there were large meat hooks hanging from the ceiling and a huge floor drain, crusted with something brown in the center of the kitchen.

Amanda also realized there were tie down straps on some of those long butcher-block counters.

She had to put one hand over her own mouth to stifle a scream.

She desperately needed to get away.

She attempted to retrace her steps, which was actually made more difficult with the lights on. Now that she could see more than that which was illuminated by the single beam dividing the darkness, she realized there were more hallways and rooms on her path. Having the lights on throughout the house also made it difficult because the paintings and sculptures along her path kept trying to pull her attention away from the task at hand. The house was stranger and more disturbing than she realized, and she was terrified of taking a wrong turn and becoming lost or, worse, trapped. Her heart pounded in her chest as she concentrated on escape. *Keep moving*, she repeated in her head over and over.

It became her mantra.

Resisting the urge to throw open the front door in relief when she found it, Amanda restrained herself and quietly opened it. She peered outside, looking for anyone or anything that would impede her hasty departure. Seeing that the way was clear, she sprinted the few yards to the car Ryley left in the driveway. Scrambling into the driver's seat and tossing the flashlight into the passenger's seat, she realized for the first time that the back of her shirt and her pants were soaked. Reaching behind her, she brought back her hand covered in blood.

Was that the pain she felt on the beach?

Was it just adrenaline allowing her to keep going?

Her questions could wait. *Keep moving.* She needed to get out of there. Luckily, Ryley had left the key in the ignition.

Amanda had never been so thankful for learning to drive a manual as she was in this moment.

"Please, please, please," she intoned, almost prayed, as she reached for the key.

She only needed a second to check the pattern of the gear shift. She realized the inside of the car was illuminated by the glow of her pendant.

Stomping on the clutch, she turned the key, bringing the engine to life. In her haste, she dumped the clutch, stalling the car. She looked up as the car shook.

That's when she saw him. Through the passenger window, not 30 feet away, the man in the red robe burst through the front door and onto the porch. Their eyes locked for just a moment, but she could clearly read his rage and ill intent.

Amanda once again pressed the clutch to the floor and turned over the engine. This time, she brought the clutch up in a smooth motion, albeit heavy on the gas. The performance engine roared as the gears caught, and she peeled out, the car fishtailing in the driveway, kicking dust and debris all around it. In the rearview mirror, through the dust, she caught sight of her pursuer coming off the porch, arms spread above his head, yelling something into the night.

She had no intention of finding out what he was saying or doing.

It felt like the very trees in the yard were leaning into the car. Limbs that had obviously been well clear from the driveway when she and Ryley came through earlier now scraped the windows. She heard the branches scrape the paint like claws as the car shot down the rapidly narrowing path.

Keep moving.

She hit third gear by the end of the driveway. As she tapped the brake at the road and downshifted, Amanda looked in her rearview mirror one last time. It appeared she had driven straight out of the woods. A clear impossibility.

In the radiance of the pendant, her eyes looked wild, unrecognizable in the rearview mirror.

Then the light from the pendant died out, and the interior of the car went dark save the very faint glow from the instrument panel. Amanda goosed the gas, slid onto the roadway, and sped off into the New Jersey night.

CHAPTER 5

How did we get separated? There was a loaded question.

Like one minute we were walking together in the park, and the next minute we were "separated" by the crowds. Not like there was a horrible gateway to another world or another dimension that physically and metaphysically ripped us apart.

I decided to skip over the chaos of the whole scene and focus on my moments, my reckoning with what happened and how we found ourselves on opposite sides of reality. Skip the blast, the awful popping sounds. Go straight for the heart of it.

Stick to the facts, McDaniel. Make it count but don't tip your hand, I thought to myself.

I took a deep drink from my wine and began my tale for Ryley. "Do you remember everyone showing up and things going sideways?"

"Vaguely. I think I was pulled away from you?" He tilted his head, and I could see he couldn't remember everything. And it bothered him. There is nothing a control freak hates more than losing the whole narrative.

"More like body tackled," I said and laughed.

He frowned. "This isn't funny, Amanda."

"Oh, I know. I was there. It was about as goddamnned unfunny as a thing can get." I had another sip of wine. "After that, there was this weird, I guess *transfer* might be the best word. An energy or something. It left the gate, went through my hands, and traveled through me. Then it rushed into my pendant. Apparently, it's been there ever since." I tried to shrug nonchalantly, but I didn't think I was succeeding. Even now, my shoulders felt stiff with the burden of my knowledge from that night.

The visions swirled through my brain again, an eddy of discord and despair, like they did during so many of my nightmares over the years. I saw the world, briefly but fatefully, through Ryley's eyes for a single moment. I saw the dark city sunken beneath the waves of the Pacific, his home, his prison. I saw these horrible creatures, men, crawling all over the land, as well as other odd beasts I didn't recognize. And I saw Ryley, in his true form, rising up from that doomed city, surveying the creatures, and feeling the hatred and contempt.

"And then?"

"Then your fam...," I caught myself, "the cultists charged me. You were sucked through the portal thing, and they started screaming. One of them rushed me, and I felt pain like someone punched me in my side."

"Which one?"

"Short skinny guy, dark hair. I have no idea who he was. I don't know their names." I frowned with the effort of recalling his angry, ugly face. "He was the only one wearing a red robe."

"Randall. He'll be the first to die. Or maybe the last. Certainly the worst death, I promise you."

I sat quietly for a moment. It was all too real. I was going to have to go back to that thrice-damned place with those goddamn lunatics. I hadn't set foot in New Jersey once since that night, despite my publisher gushing over an opportunity for me to give an invited lecture at Princeton. Teenaged Me would have been thrilled. Traumatized Me passed on it without a second thought.

I'd rather never write another book than cross the Hudson. Now, it might be the last place I'd ever see in this lifetime. Goddamn Jersey.

"He punched you. Go on. What else happened? I need to know so I can, so we can lift the madness, as you said."

"But it wasn't a punch, Ryley. It was a knife. That little prick stabbed me with some ceremonial dagger. I could feel a sort of odd pressure," I put my hand over my side, "then the cold as the hilt stopped at my skin. So fucking cold. The pain snapped me out of my inertia. I pushed away from the gate and, it was weird. It was like the light emanating from it...broke?" My voice did that upturn at the end of a sentence that one associates with questions. How do you explain light falling away from an object and breaking like a mirror? That's not a thing that can happen.

"The light. It, like, shattered. Into a million pieces. Then they, I mean the cultists, really started howling. I bolted out of there as fast as I could." I rubbed my side absently, reliving the wound, the feeling of that metal sliding into my skin, the cultist tugging viciously, serrating my skin, organs popping like balloons at a child's party. At least, that's what it feels like in my mind when I wake up screaming in the middle of the night, envisioning all of the grotesque details, real or imagined. I can't understand why my unconscious mind insists on reliving that horror over and over again, but it certainly does. Over and over and over again.

"Can I see?" His request was tender, devoid of his usual anger.

I stood and untied my sash, letting the robe fall open. I stepped closer, turned slightly away from him, and indicated the scar on my right side. Looking out the window, I tried to detach from the reminder of my body's abuse as Ryley ran his finger slowly over the jagged streak on my skin, grey and shiny, still slightly puffy after all these years.

I felt him lean over and kiss the scar almost reverently. He dropped a half-dozen kisses down the length of it. Then he pulled me between his legs and gently laid the side of his face against my stomach, holding me close. His warm hands ran up and down the backs of my thighs in a tender gesture I wasn't sure he had been capable of making. Its genuineness shook me more than his incendiary anger at the cultist.

"I won't let them hurt you ever again, my Morningstar. I should have protected you."

Pulling away so I could hold his face between my hands, I bent down to touch my forehead to his, my pendant swinging dangerously close to him.

"But you did protect me." I brushed aside his hair and kissed his forehead. Taking his hands in mine, I sat down again, my robe still open to him. "When I got back to the car, you'd left the keys in the ignition. And when I looked down at my hand, all that blood, I thought I would die. But I didn't. The pendant was glowing when I got back to the car, and there was no longer a gaping hole in my side, just that scar. In fifteen years, that pendant has never once glowed again."

"That snap I got today tells me it's still potent, though."

"Just because it's not glowing doesn't mean it's not working." I pulled up the chain and ran my fingers across the shell's imperfect surface. "It's you in here, Ryley. Your essence. Your power. You may have been gone for fifteen years, but I've always carried a part of you with me."

I felt like this was as close as Ryley and I could be emotionally. It was time to make my pitch.

"But the madness is too much, Ry. Too much for a mere mortal like me, I suppose. I can't take it anymore. Yes, my pendant protects me, but if I wasn't being chased by cultists, I wouldn't need protection." I ran my fingers over the little shell's bumps, as familiar to me as a friend. "This pendant warps everything it touches."

"Even you?" Ryley asked.

I frowned. "Maybe. I don't know. It literally drives anyone close to me insane."

"Sanity is overrated," Ryley smiled at his own joke. He'd seen the saying on a t-shirt once and seemed to think it was the wittiest thing ever.

"It's not funny. Look, right after," I waved my hand, "all of this happened, I went back to my old life, as best as I could. I mean, we'd graduated, so I moved off campus. I had some money set aside from some birthday checks that I think came from my biological dad. I tried to get on with my life."

"Without me."

"Yes, without you. What choice did I have?" I poured the last of the second bottle into my glass, only getting enough to wet the bottom.

Uncharacteristically, Ryley actually got up to get the third bottle. He opened it and poured it for both of us.

"I understand, Amanda. You didn't have a choice."

"Thank you," I said, gesturing to the wine. "Anyway, I got a job at a small publishing house and wrote nearly every other waking minute. I got three roommates, and we split a small apartment in the Bronx. I was sort of living the life I'd always imagined when I was growing up. But then the madness seeped in."

"Nightmares?"

"For me? Oh, yeah. All the time in those first few months. I must've looked like hell from the bags under my eyes. But it really hit my roommates hard." I swirled the wine in my glass, remembering when I began to notice the abhorrent behavior of the people around me and the chaos leaching into my life.

"I was writing, of course. Submitting short stories and eventually book manuscripts. I got lucky because almost everything sold, even if it wasn't for a lot of money. Ten dollars here. Twenty dollars and contributor's copies there. Then, on my 21st birthday, I got what turned out to be my last birthday check, as well as a check and a note congratulating me on graduating from NYU. It was thousands of dollars."

"I take it that's a lot of money?"

I chuckled. "Yes, Ryley. Especially when you are a starving artist. It's a shit ton of money."

He frowned when I laughed at him, but I couldn't help it. Every time I started to think of Ryley as human, he reminded me that he wasn't. The normal cares or concerns of an average person were not his cares or concerns.

"Anyway, I had the best life. I got up every morning, walked to the train, stopping at a little deli on the way for a breakfast sandwich and coffee. I'd spend all day on other people's stories, reading all of this wonderful work. I hit a bodega every night on the way home for a sandwich. Then I'd come home and write until I fell asleep. It was perfect."

"But?"

I thought about my time at the apartment. The rush of going out on my own, away from the dorms, away from family. It was just me and the city. I really didn't interact with my roommates a lot, especially at first. We were just four people splitting rent and a tiny living space, each with our own lives and routines. But within a few months, they started coming to me, one by one, to talk about, well, nonsense stuff and dark dreams they kept having. It was like they didn't want to talk to me, but they were compelled to talk to me, to tell me everything.

It's not like anyone ever really wants to listen to someone else's dreams; although everyone is dying to share their own, this was different. They looked haunted as they came to me, at first sporadically and then daily, to tell me about their night terrors. Some were vague, just sensations of being suffocated, of drowning, of struggling to get to a dark shore and having waves wash over them, pulling them back into the depths of the ocean. Some were specific: descriptions of nightmarish creatures roaming about in unreal landscapes, impressions of being an ant in a city built to scale for giants. Others' dreams were more esoteric, like feelings of a haunting doom that was so close, just over their shoulder, breathing down their neck, their every hair rigidly at attention, their skin tingling with dread - only to turn and see... nothing.

I'm a little embarrassed to admit, even to myself, that I used those talking sessions as fodder for my stories. And I certainly wouldn't admit it out loud to Ryley. I thought about those first few years in the Bronx. Shout out to Dickens: the best of times and the worst of times. While everything had felt idyllic on some days, watching everyone around me unravel was a unique and awful experience.

"There's more Ryley. So much more. The editor I worked with transferred overseas on almost no notice. He said he had to get as far from New York as he could. Weird graffiti started popping up on walls along my workday travel route. Symbols, like I saw on the gate in New Jersey, were painted on the side-walk or tagged on buildings. Every now and then, when I went to the deli, one of the people behind the counter would say some-thing to me in a weird language, and when I asked them about it, they would deny saying anything. The bodega cat wouldn't let me pet her after a few months, and I was a regular. It was all really weird. It was like the whole world was trying to gaslight me. So, when I put together enough money and sold enough books, I bought a place in Connecticut and moved away to be alone."

Ryley was unusually patient and thoughtful as I told him my tale of woe.

"You gave up your dream of living in New York City," he said. "It's so unlike you to give up on anything."

"I just couldn't take the way I seemed to be affecting everyone around me. It was like I was torturing them."

"You were always so soft-hearted, Morningstar."

"It's not 'soft-hearted,'" I said, making air quotes around his criticism, and with him, that would definitely be a criticism. "It's basic human decency."

Ryley made a sound that was just short of a grunt. He didn't think much of humanity or the idea of being a part of it. Decency was definitely a foreign concept to him, a relic of a world he wanted wiped away.

"Anyway, Connecticut was close enough to commute back to the city on a whim and far enough that I could be alone. I picked up a gorgeous beach house. I got lucky as the previous owner dumped it for a song. You'd love it. Light wood, lots of windows, nautical theme throughout. And it's got a spectacular kitchen. Everywhere you look outside, it's a curated yard, a beach, or the ocean itself."

"Sounds nice," he said with little enthusiasm.

I couldn't find a way to make domesticity sound interesting to him. He didn't understand that any more than he understood humanity. He certainly didn't understand the thrill I'd had choosing and purchasing something that was truly mine. A home. A *real* home.

"Yeah, it is nice. I mean, it was."

"Until?"

"My mother."

"Ah."

"My mom and her new husband moved up to Connecticut to live with me."

Ryley's eyes got huge. "She got married?"

I nodded. "A guy named Tucker. And I have a half-sister named Luella that lives in Sarasota. I met her once. She seemed nice. Oh, and I have a half-brother named, I shit you not, Cletus."

"Is that a strange name for a man?" Ryley cocked his head.

"It just means I completed my trailer trash Bingo card."

"I don't know what any of that means," Ryley said, looking completely earnest and a little baffled.

"It means my mother did just about what everyone had expected of her. She married a guy she met at a bar and moved into his trailer. But Tucker didn't think it was fair that a famous author's mother and her stepfather should have to live," I dropped my voice low to imitate Tucker, "'in a crappy, double-wide in a fucking burg outside-a Pensacola.'"

I returned to my normal voice. "Never mind that it was his crappy trailer."

"So, they moved in with you?"

"What can I say? I gave in. She slathered on the guilt, and I gave in. To top it all off, once she got there, she hated every-thing, and I mean *everything* about Connecticut. And she let me know it."

"Kick her out," he said with a shrug.

"I would have an easier time getting rid of bedbugs."

"Ah, so your mother is an infestation."

"Absolutely."

CHAPTER 6

Ten Years Ago

A manda felt like everything was going great.

Until her mom and Tucker moved in with her.

Amanda hadn't wanted the intrusion, and she did everything she could to stave it off. The only thing she wouldn't do, and Caroline pressured her repeatedly, was to send a monthly stipend to Florida for Caroline and Tucker. Her mom said it wasn't fair that she had supported Amanda for 20 years – *barely 18*, Amanda thought, *but who was counting?* – only to have Amanda abandon her in Florida. Besides, Tucker didn't think it was right for a famous author's mother to live in a trailer park in Pensacola. "What would people think?" was his constant mantra.

Caroline and Tucker persisted in that they were not to be denied their place in what they thought would be an East Coast royal court of famous authors hanging around and doing famous author things together. Despite the fact that Amanda didn't know any other authors, had no friends to speak of and wrote under the pseudonym M.S. McDaniel, they had their fanciful daydreams.

No one she interacted with day-to-day had any idea who she was, and she really liked it that way.

She highly doubted either her mom or Tucker had ever read a book, even hers, so she wasn't sure what authors they were thinking would befriend them. Despite that, they moved to Connecticut to live with Amanda.

The first few months of their "extended visit" went as well as Amanda could have hoped. Her mother swanned around in what Amanda called "faux Palm Beach chic," a joke her mother didn't understand, but one that nonetheless pissed off Caroline every time Amanda mentioned it. Caroline wore all-white pantsuits and chunky white wedges, even during winter months. Not the fashion icon his wife was, Tucker dressed the way he thought a gentleman of leisure should: in jeans and a t-shirt, with high-end stores' flannels, and his signature Gators trucker hat. Caroline had bought him some fancy clothes, but they'd only lasted a few weeks before the t-shirts from the local bars came out. At least he was comfortable, and he steadfastly ignored Caroline's shrill commands to dress up. Amanda admired that.

Tucker and Caroline had only been in Connecticut for a few months when their mental health appeared to deteriorate. After the horrible situation with her roommates, Amanda was on the lookout for trouble, and she was certain it had found her again.

At first, it seemed like explainable things. Irritability. Short tempers. Sleepwalking, although Amanda never remembered her mother sleepwalking before. She did notice that her mom became intermittently "squirrely," but that didn't seem too far off from her norm. Tucker seemed particularly agitated all the time, but she didn't know him well enough to decide if that was normal or not.

Amanda knew she had to find a solution after a particularly rough night.

It was a lovely fall day, and Amanda had just finished her novel, *Underworld Reign*, a whole three days before deadline.

She was able to work, in part, because her mom and Tucker had been out all day at some car racing event at Lime Rock Park. She was ecstatic. To celebrate, she ordered a white clam pizza and a Seaside Special – a no-sauce pizza loaded with bacon, clams, shrimp, and lobster – from her favorite local pizzeria, had them delivered, and popped open a bottle of oaked chardonnay that she'd saved for exactly this occasion.

Amanda took the time to set her place at her table. She had an antique silver, five-branched candelabra she'd found at a local estate sale, and she placed fresh beeswax sticks into its holders. She uncorked her wine and poured a glass. She lit the candles. She put her favorite Veer Union CD into the stereo and started it. When the pizzas arrived, she was ready.

She placed the pizzas on her dining room table, enjoying the smell of her prize. It was like walking into a fancy seafood restaurant, and it set her stomach to growling. After living in New York City for a few years and enjoying a great slice on demand, Amanda hadn't believed she would love Connecticut's signature white clam pizza so damn much. She'd never once in her life thought to put clams on a pizza, but once she started, she couldn't stop. She was ruined for other pizzas. It was salty with a bite, creamy and garlicky. It was also the gateway drug to the Seaside Special. They were like fresh seafood dinners served on crispy, cheesy garlic bread. Although they were spendy, she felt momentous occasions, such as finishing her work-in-progress, warranted such opulence. She started with one slice of each and savored every bite. She was in heaven.

Unfortunately, not ten minutes into her repast, with her favorite music wafting through her stereo, the food and music nourishing her soul, Caroline and Tucker returned home in the midst of a fight and a slamming of doors.

"I can't believe we had to spend all day at the track, Tucker. I'm filthy, just filthy. This outfit's just ruined with dust. Now I gotta buy a new one again. And that means I gotta ask Amanda for more money again, and…" Caroline paused midsentence when they came all the way into the house and saw Amanda sitting at the dining room table by candlelight. "Oh. I thought you were writing." She squinted suspiciously at the candles. "You got a man here?"

Tucker barreled into the dining room right behind her and flipped on the light, making Amanda flinch from the sudden illumination.

Tucker snorted. "Shit. Like she'd have a man, period. She ain't never had a man. College boyfriend, my ass. Bet he weren't even real. You ever seen his picture, Carrie? You ever meet 'im? Hah! A man." He shook his head and plopped down at the table in the seat right next to Amanda. "Hey, pizza! I'm starvin'! Babe, get me a couple a beers." He grabbed two slices from Amanda's Seaside Special, folding it into one slice and jamming it into his mouth. "This fish shit is gross. Why don't you get a real pizza for a change? Like pepperoni and shit."

Amanda glared as a huge chunk of lobster fell from Tucker's pizza sandwich and hit the table with a buttery plop. She could barely contain her disgust as he scooped it up with his grubby hand and shoved it in his maw.

"If you don't like my pizza, why don't you go get your own?" Amanda ground out from between her teeth.

"I told you I was fuckin' hungry. You deaf, too? Damn, girl."

Caroline appeared from the kitchen with a six-pack of beer and set it down next to her husband. Amanda noted it was actually her local craft beer, not Tucker's usual swill. Caroline was also holding a huge wine glass, which she filled with Amanda's chardonnay.

"Help yourself, Mom."

Caroline ignored her, blew out the candles, and moved the candelabra to the far end of the table. She returned to the place next to Amanda and across from Tucker and sat down.

"Why don't you ever get a normal pizza? This stuff is weird."

The irony was completely lost on Caroline as she also grabbed two slices, folded them, and started eating. She pulled up the box and ate hunched over it, with toppings dripping into it.

Amanda completely lost her appetite. She refilled her wine glass, went into the living room, and turned off her stereo. Her mom and Tucker ruined her small but significant piece of relaxation. She moved to the windows to look out over the ocean. The nearly floor-to-ceiling windows felt like direct portals to the water, minus the chill breeze outside. She could see a ship in the distance, its light steadily moving across the horizon. This view was one of the few things that brought her peace and even a peculiar sense of belonging. Despite the feeling of solitude that usually accompanied her watch, she was keenly aware of her mom and Tucker still in her house. Even a room away, she could clearly hear everything transpiring in the dining room.

For a few minutes, the only sounds were of Caroline and Tucker eating, as well as the popping and slurping of cans of beer, punctuated by frequent belches. Amanda also heard her bottle of wine clunking down onto the table at least twice. Eventually, the eating slowed. Caroline and Tucker took that opportunity to resume the fight they put on hold when they arrived.

Apparently, it wasn't just about the track.

What Amanda found odd, as she was practically forced to eavesdrop due to her proximity, was that, although they were both raising their voices to ever-greater volumes, they seemed to be arguing for the *same thing*. She listened as they shouted back and forth that they needed an apartment in the city, that Amanda should be paying for it, that she should cover their other expenses as well.

"It's not fair!" Caroline wailed.

"Damn right, it's not fair. I don't see why you can't understand that!" Tucker countered.

"You don't know! She should just pay for everything. It'd be so much better if she weren't so cheap! Why's she so horrible to me?"

"She more horrible to me! Ungrateful bitch. After I took care of her mama after she deserted her."

It was just getting to the point that Amanda thought she would have to cut them both off to keep the neighbors from calling the police. Even with so much space between the houses, the screaming was bound to carry on a crisp night. Then it was silent for a few seconds, and the argument changed. She heard the dining chairs scrape along the floor and some odd thumps.

"Ia! Ia! C'ch'ph'phlegeth!" Caroline intoned in a high-pitched voice.

"C's'uhn tharanak Cthulhu li'hee n'gha!" Tucker boomed in a deep voice, far deeper than his usual timbre and with no trace of his Florida Panhandle accent.

Amanda rushed back to her dining room to find the battling couple had descended into madness. Caroline stood barefoot on the table, her chunky wedges resting next to her feet. Tucker held the newly relit candelabra and was jabbing it at Caroline from his position below her. Caroline, for her part, seemed to be doing nothing to dodge the flames or her clearly insane husband. She made buzzy noises, bombinating with her hands raised to the sky, as Tucker tried to light her shirt on fire.

"Tucker! What in the hell are you doing?"

At Amanda's shriek, both players froze in place like guilty children caught in an illicit act. Caroline ceased to buzz, but her eyes shifted down to stare at Amanda. They were blank with a total lack of awareness. The absurdity of it left Amanda stunned. None of the three of them moved until Caroline's shirt finally caught. Then Amanda moved quickly, dousing her mother with the remainder of her wine, reaching up to rip the shirt from her.

Amanda stomped it on the floor, smothering the last of the flames.

Both Caroline and Tucker blinked stupidly, and Caroline stepped down off of the table. Tucker sat with a thud, slamming the candelabra to the table, dislodging one candle. The candle dropped to the table and sputtered out. Caroline stood mute before Amanda, unashamed or uncaring about her disheveled, half-undressed state.

"What did you say up there?" Amanda asked Caroline, shaking with anger and spent adrenaline.

"I...I don't," Caroline trailed off without finishing.

Amanda turned to Tucker. "When I was in the other room, what the fuck did you say?"

"I said," he paused, looking very confused. "I took care of your mama when you left?"

"After that," Amanda snarled.

"I don't know."

His voice was small. He appeared to retreat within himself. He'd flushed bright red since plopping down in the chair, whether from embarrassment or exertion, Amanda couldn't tell, nor could she be bothered to care.

"Go to your rooms. Do not come back out until at least tomorrow morning."

"I'm not a child, Amanda Melissa McDaniel, and I will not be spoken to like..."

"I said, 'Go!'" Amanda thundered.

"But my clothes," Caroline whined, gesturing at her sooty pants and nearly unrecognizable shirt on the floor.

Amanda put one hand up to silence her mother, pointed in the direction of their rooms, grabbed the bottle with her remaining wine, and stalked out, heading for the living room to go out onto the balcony.

Just before she got out of earshot, she heard Tucker say, "That's the kind shit we shouldn't have to put up with."

The whole situation had set off a headache with a force she hadn't felt since before she'd moved to Connecticut. It took several deep breaths of ocean air to calm her quaking nerves. She closed her eyes, inhaled the essence of the sea, and rubbed her pendant to soothe herself until the headache receded.

She stood out there most of the night, uncaring about the cool breezes blowing across her skin, turning it to gooseflesh. When she finished her wine, she tossed the bottle down toward the beach, relishing in the sound of glass smashing on the rocks below. She needed more time and more privacy. She craved solitude. She also saw her roommate experience in the Bronx replaying itself with her mom and Tucker. And Tucker could've killed her mother and burned down the house tonight. They needed some distance.

Amanda needed them to have some distance.

The following day, she sent her mom and Tucker on vacation. She'd ordered a car for them and arranged for them to spend a few days in the city while she figured out their next destination. She enjoyed the quiet so much; she made sure their bags were never unpacked for more than a month or two at a time after that.

Sending them off to travel seemed to help. Amanda paid for trips for the two of them, gladly buying a little peace and quiet for herself. Her mother wanted to be a world traveler. After she and Tucker got passports, they toured Europe. After the first grand tour, they would just pop over to one country or another and spend a week. They stuck with countries where English was the language of the land. From what Amanda could tell from her credit card bills, these visits were mostly to stay in nice hotels while eating at American fast food joints. There was always some clothes shopping, but not much in the way of seeing museums or enjoying restaurants beyond where they could have eaten within twenty miles of the house. Her mother treated Europe like a mall without the parking lots.

When it was Tucker's turn to choose their travel destination, he preferred to stay stateside. They attended sports events when he had his way. They saw the Kentucky Derby, which gave Caroline an excuse to buy a ridiculous Derby hat and to drink mint juleps until she puked. Caroline was nothing if not classy. They didn't even get to see the Run for the Roses because, by the time they started the race itself, Caroline was in the building being cared for by EMTs due to her excessive intoxication.

After three blissful years of intermittent travel, however, they once again declared they wanted their own place in the city and an allowance. Basically, Caroline's view of New York City was informed almost entirely by TV shows. She wanted a place on Fifth Avenue, which Amanda couldn't afford. In addition, she still wanted to be able to travel. Amanda thought she had shut it down by saying no repeatedly and quite forcefully.

By that time, even travel didn't seem to be enough to calm whatever mental issues were festering in Caroline and Tucker. Caroline would walk into a room, seeming to be talking to someone who wasn't there. It became apparent that she was rehashing and reliving pieces of her past. She would slip and call Tucker "Dominique," which would piss him off so bad, he wouldn't speak to her for days at a time. She would wake up in the night screaming. Tucker said she must have gone to the Playboy Mansion at some point because she talked about men in robes in her sleep.

Tucker was an idiot.

But he was also misinformed about Caroline's past, which was part of the reason that he came up with increasingly wild theories about her mutterings and her behavior. Amanda didn't think she'd ever given him the whole story of how Amanda came to be in the first place. Hell, Amanda herself was still piecing it together after all these years.

Since she'd been old enough to apply critical thinking skills, Amanda had been skeptical of her mother's original story about her biological father. Like any kid would, when Amanda had been old enough to realize that most of her friends had a dad in their lives, she asked why she didn't have one. Caroline spun a fairy tale about a handsome young man from a very rich family that fell in love with Caroline when they met at the beach. The story included salacious details about their torrid summer love affair that certainly wasn't age-appropriate the first several times Amanda heard it. The basic narrative was that Caroline's dashing young suitor went off to college, and his parents forbade him from returning to Florida to marry Caroline. He never even knew she was pregnant when he left. Caroline would often wistfully add a slight sigh for her true love lost. Amanda's first clue that this story wasn't accurate came in the form of changing details, including Mr. Handsome's name. Sometimes it was Shaun, and sometimes it was Chad, and sometimes Caroline would say his name wasn't the important part. The important part was that Shaun/Chad loved her and that he never would have left her had he known she was pregnant. The important part to Caroline, as always, was Caroline. This contradictory information was frustrating to Amanda, and Caroline stopped answering questions about it altogether when Amanda left for college. Now, however, the story was making a reappearance in a new and terrifying form.

In between whining about wanting their own place in the city and pleading for money, Caroline started experiencing serious anger issues. She began lashing out at Amanda, and slowly the real story of Amanda's birth and the mystery checks Amanda had received over the years came out. Over the past few months, Amanda had learned she was the result of a one night stand on an alcohol-soaked road trip to Mardi Gras. When Amanda was born, the checks arrived out of the blue, and Caroline was left to raise Amanda without any emotional assistance. Now Caroline didn't even try to work with the old story anymore. There appeared to be more sympathy to be gained from this new angle than there was to be wrung out from the old version, but she still didn't like Amanda's questions that put the focus back on the mystery father. Having even snippets of the truth out in the open made them both uncomfortable.

With this shift in the dynamics of their shared history, their mother-daughter relationship became even more strained. Every time Amanda pressed for details, Caroline got angry. Caroline's outbursts spiraled out of control, and Amanda contracted with a local "wellness spa" for Caroline to take a month's rest and get some mental care. Not wanting to remain in the house alone with Tucker, she gifted him with a first-class airplane ticket to visit his daughter, Luella, who lived in Sarasota.

For four weeks, Amanda reveled in the peace and quiet of her roommate-free home. She wrote, ate leisurely meals in her own dining room, and enjoyed the freedom of being able to lounge around the house all day in nothing but her robe. Things even seemed smooth for a few weeks once Caroline and Tucker were both back, but eventually, Caroline ramped up even more than before she went away. It seemed that the craziness picked up where it left off, so it escalated quickly once they returned. Caroline renewed her call for financial support and their own place.

"Why won't you get me and Tucker a nice place in the city?" Caroline whined. "Someplace fun. Connecticut is so boring. There ain't nothing fun to do, and all the people around here are old and have big sticks up their ass. I hate it. It's awful."

She gave a little foot stomp for good measure.

Amanda pinched the bridge of her nose. Of course, leave it to her mother to miss the irony of seeing herself standing in front of a floor-to-ceiling window overlooking the ocean on a gorgeous, sunny day and complaining about the accommodations. Amanda felt a headache coming on. Her mother often had that effect on her.

"I want to go to the city where it's exciting. There's movie and TV stars there, too. If I wanted to be around regular, boring old people, I'd a stayed in Florida." Caroline certainly sounded like she was straight out of the trailer park, but she was decked out in her Palm Beach uniform, white pantsuit, and wedges, flouting the rule about wearing white after Labor Day. She insisted on a full manicure twice a week and wearing makeup every day. Amanda thought she looked like an extra from an 80s nighttime soap, big blown-out hair and all.

"You could have stayed in Florida. It's not like I invited you to stay here. You invited yourself. And Tucker," Amanda reminded her.

"Well, it's just shitty to leave me and Tucker in some dumpy trailer park when you are a rich, successful author. That's just mean." Caroline added a pout to her repertoire.

"I'm not rich, Mom. And that 'dumpy' trailer park was actually pretty nice. Didn't Tucker own that double-wide?"

"The trailer park was awful," Caroline said, drawing out the last word for emphasis. "You have a big, fancy house on the beach."

"Which you just said you hated."

"That seems pretty damn rich to me." Caroline threw Amanda a dirty look for catching her in her hypocrisy.

"You and Tucker already have your own wing of the house. You've got two rooms, your own master bathroom, and a small courtyard. It's probably more space than you had in the whole trailer."

"But it's booorring." Caroline extended the word like a sullen teenager. She included an appropriate eyeroll and a crossing of her arms to go with her mood.

"Maybe you and Tucker could take another trip," Amanda offered, silently calculating how much that might cost her, depending upon whether her mom or Tucker picked the destination.

Amanda hoped it was Tucker's turn. She'd lost track.

"I gave up everything for you, Amanda Melissa McDaniel. Everything!"

Great. It was going to be this tactic again. Only recently, her mom had become increasingly weird about her past, letting slip details that she hadn't shared before. Amanda wasn't really comfortable with the new additions to the old stories.

"Why, I was only 15 when..."

Amanda cut her off. "I know. Snuck out of the house. Road trip. Mardi Gras. Me nine months later. I know."

"Dominique was so handsome." Caroline's eyes glassed over, and she slipped into a strange voice, almost childlike.

It gave Amanda the creeps. This was another chapter in the story. Amanda played along.

"Dominique? Who is Dominique?"

"Why, certainly, I'd love to go back to your place. As long as we can keep the party rollin', sugar." Caroline appeared to be talking to someone, but it was like Amanda wasn't even in the room anymore.

"Your house is ugly! Yuck! Whadaya mean everyone does that? Let the place look rundown to protect it from thieves? Seems you'd want it to look nice. Mason Boocanyay? Who's Mason? Is that your dad? You people have some weird names."

Amanda watched as Caroline appeared to step through a gate or door that wasn't there, taking an invisible hand for assistance.

"Oh, this is much nicer inside! Desi is gonna be so jealous that she had to sleep in the car again!"

Caroline appeared to be drinking invisible shooters, giggling, and flirting with a man who wasn't there.

"Yeah, I've been waiting all night for you to ask." Caroline sauntered across the room and sat down hard on Amanda's living room couch. She reclined and began writhing and moaning.

"Mom! Mom, that's enough. Come on. Snap out of it," Amanda called across the room. She didn't want to touch her mother or be near her with whatever was going on right now.

"Oh, Dominique. I do want to, yes. God, yes." Caroline was moaning. Suddenly, she sat straight up, covering her chest as if in modesty. "Oh my God! Who are these people? What are they saying? I don't... I mean, I thought that..."

Amanda watched, horrified, as Caroline relaxed and rested back on the cushions.

"No, we still can. It's okay. I still want to do what you want to do, okay? It's good. No one else is here. It's good. If you say so. I don't even see them anymore. It's like..."

Then she commenced to chanting, rhythmically thrusting her hips with her own beat. "*Stellam matutinam,* the keeper and the gate. *Stellam matutinam,* the keeper, and the gate. Call him forth to you, O Keeper of the Gate!"

Caroline continued her grotesque pantomime, picking up speed with her chant and breathing heavily, panting between lines. She writhed in ecstasy, her manicured nails clawing and ripping the fabric in her grip. Amanda found herself stunned and embarrassed to watch her mother full-on orgasm.

Suddenly, Caroline sat bolt upright, fingers still dug into the couch.

"...I had you. I didn't have any friends. My family disowned me. You cost me everything. I mean everything, Amanda. It's just not fair." She blinked a few times and pulled her fingers free. "Why did you make me sit down?"

"You looked tired," Amanda replied, still shaken. This was the worst episode yet. And there was less and less time between them. She was even more alarmed by her mother's behavior, but now she had three names for her research: Dominique, Mason Boocanyay, and *stellam matutinam*. Since Dominique was a French name, she was going to assume that her mom's pronunciation was a bastardization of something French as well. Boucanier, maybe? Buccaneer? Combined with what sounded like Latin, Amanda was very confused, but she committed every syllable to memory for her notes.

"I am tired. Tired of fighting with you over this." Caroline stood up shakily. "I'm going to my room to take a nap. Then I am getting packed."

"Packed?"

"You said I should take a vacation. I think I am going to do just that." Caroline made a huge showing of crossing the room toward her wing. "I hear Southern Italy is nice this time of year."

Great, Amanda thought.

Just her luck. It wasn't Tucker's turn, after all.

CHAPTER 7

"Where's your mom now?" Ryley's voice was deceptively gentle. He'd never met my mother, but I hadn't painted him the most flattering picture of her either.

I blinked a few times, holding back the memories and some tears. "A very exclusive spa for her mental wellness. It costs a fortune, but it's worth it to know they'll take care of her."

I thought about when I had signed in my mom at her latest retreat. She flounced around like Blanche DuBois in *A Streetcar Named Desire*. It was all I could do to get her into my loungewear that morning, so there she was, disheveled and decked out in fuzzy octopus jammies. She desperately flirted with the orderly and called him Dominique as they took her away. This was going to be a long visit.

I shook myself to throw off the bad vibes of that whole horrible ordeal and reflexively closed my robe for protection.

"And Tucker?"

Tucker was faring no better. In the final week before I'd sent them both away, I'd caught him having in-depth, heartfelt conversations with the corners of rooms around my house and once an argument with a potted ficus in my foyer. The symphony he conducted in front of my refrigerator was a slight to behold, as was his naked midnight serenade of an oak tree in my yard. Tucker was a big fan of inanimate object interaction.

"He can fucking rot for all I care. He just married my mom to sponge off her 'famous author daughter.' I had him committed at a local mental health hospital in New Haven."

Ryley reassessed me after my abrupt turn to anger. I could tell he was trying to figure out how to proceed. He went with the tactic of changing the subject. A classic.

Smart man.

"You've mentioned being an author a few times now. Wasn't that always your dream?"

Really, it had been. Ever since I was little, I'd wanted to be a writer. I wrote stories and read them to my stuffed animals. I wrote your typical sappy teenaged poetry that filled reams of notebooks, most of which I had boxed up. I never wanted anyone to read those works, but I was strangely protective of them none-theless.

"It was. It was why I majored in Writing at college." I got up and cut myself a slice of cake and one for Ryley. "After you, uh, left, I started writing in the horror genre, and it just clicked. It turns out my life was perfectly suited to it."

I turned back to give Ryley his cake and found him staring at me.

"You consider me a horror?" Ryley tilted his head as he asked. It was a disarmingly human gesture. He actually looked hurt.

"No, not you, of course not you," I reassured the god who usually slumbered beneath the waves. That which was dead but could not die. I focused on seeing him as human, as the man I had loved, so I could reassure him. "But some of our experiences in New Jersey really lend themselves to fiction."

I paused a moment to read his reaction. "Besides, the agency and publishers thought that was the genre that would sell more books."

Now it was my turn to proceed cautiously. I tried to tiptoe around the subject, but the fact was that Ryley was the source of my horror and most of my damage. He was a god and not a benign one. The horrific things I saw through that gate haunted me. After that night, I'd wake up screaming from night terrors. I'd catch myself daydreaming about those awful people, that writhing sea, and I would snap out of it drenched in sweat. It wasn't like I could go to a therapist and tell my tale, not unless I wanted to be involuntarily committed. Writing became my therapy. Writing was cathartic for me. The only way I could cope with what happened was to fictionalize it and write it away.

He stood up and walked around behind me, the fingers of his left hand trailing along the collar of my robe. He stood behind me and leaned down to breathe into my ear.

"Am I in your books, Amanda? Some evil come to destroy mankind." Ryley went from hurt to angry at top speed. I couldn't tell if he meant to be menacing or enticing, but the combination of both was intoxicating. Dancing along that knife's edge had always been an aphrodisiac for me.

I stood up, moved around the chair, and kissed him hard. I kissed him with every bit of passion in me. I kissed him with 15 years of fear, rage, and pent-up desire. I kissed him and willed him to understand me.

I needed to defuse the situation before I completely offended him. Also, he wasn't in any of my books. I could never bring myself to fictionalize him. He was mine. My burden to bear; my Ryley to love. I wouldn't share him with anyone else.

I pulled away from our embrace.

"I can assure you. I would never portray you like that. Never."

I reached out and held his face between my hands. "I swear to you," I said, looking him directly in the eyes and watching his anger drain away. "My stories involve mad cultists and monsters. Horrors made by man and creatures made by magic. Not you. And not us."

He paused a moment longer, and I took the opportunity to enjoy being able to nakedly gaze at his face. I wanted to memorize every curve of his jaw. The set of his eyes and their magnificent aquamarine color. When we first got together, I asked him if he wore contacts. The color seemed too vivid to be natural, and I guess, in a way, they really weren't. Natural, I mean. Ryley wasn't really natural. He was otherworldly, literally. But those stunning eyes conjured visions of a Caribbean bay or a glacier-fed river. Hot and cold, just like Ryley.

Ryley smiled, took my hands, and tugged me gently toward the bedroom.

"Come back to bed, Morningstar. Let's make good memories in tonight's darkness while we can."

And we did.

The following morning, I woke up snuggled next to Ryley. I had the privilege of watching him for a few minutes as he continued to sleep. I watched the gentle rise and fall of his chest. Enjoyed the peaceful look on his face. Everything about Ryley sleeping was calm and relaxed, the diametric opposite of Ryley awake. Sure, he often tried to exhibit a calm demeanor, but he was a control freak, as one might expect of an alien god. Nobody had to tell me, least of all Ryley himself, that he felt vulnerable without his powers.

As the caretaker of his powers, tucked safely in my pendant for more than fifteen years, I kind of knew how he felt. For me, although I could not access the godlike powers in my little nautilus shell, I could feel them, like a low-key vibration against my chest. When I wrote, they kept me company, resonating inspiration, and encouragement. They were my muse, my very own personalized divine. I would feel naked without them, and I had several thousand fewer years to adjust to them. I could only imagine how hard it was for Ryley.

I sat up carefully, making sure not to give him an accidental zap from my pendant or chain. Although the pendant never glowed after that first time when it healed me, it did shock anyone who touched it, apparently even Ryley. That would be a rude awakening for him. But as I rose up, Ryley stirred. He yawned and stretched his full length limbs over the edge of the bed. He blinked the morning sun out of his eyes and reached for me.

"No, 's early," he mumbled. "Come back to bed."

He tried to catch ahold of my arm, but I pulled away. I wanted to make a joke about him being a slugabed, or Rip Van Winkle, or something clever, but I didn't think I could risk it without offending him. He was always touchy about the subject of sleep. If I was going to have his cooperation with the ritual, I would need him happy and on my side. Instead of risking turning his mood sour first thing in the morning, I just smiled as I let our fingers slide slowly apart.

Heading to the bathroom, I realized I was sore from a night of using muscles I'd forgotten I had. I blushed a little at the memories. Returning to the bedroom in my big, fluffy hotel robe, I sat on the edge of Ryley's side of the bed. He was face down in his pillow, but I knew he hadn't fallen back to sleep. I gently rubbed his back, the way I used to wake him up in college. Before, well, everything.

He finally rolled over to face me.

"It's gotta be today, doesn't it?" He ran his hand up my arm as he spoke.

"'Fraid so. Stars are right."

"The stars are going to have to wait a little bit. I'm hungry again. Can't face destiny on an empty stomach."

He reached out for the quaint landline on the bed stand, the direct line to our butler, and ordered enough breakfast for an entourage, a veritable banquet.

"And I also want Devils on Horseback and deviled eggs. And champagne."

He hung up the phone.

"Since we have a few minutes, I think getting cleaned up is in order." He waggled his eyebrows at me. "Have you seen the shower in there? Plenty of room for two."

He sat up and slowly pulled my robe apart, kissing my skin as the robe revealed me to him. After an impromptu round of morning sex in the bed, he carried me into the shower to go again.

I'd missed Ryley's sense of fun and his inhuman levels of stamina. Might as well enjoy it all while I could, I thought.

He finally let me out of the shower, and we both lounged in our robes until breakfast arrived. Along with our own personal breakfast buffet was a neat package with Ryley's cleaned clothes inside. It was only 9:00 am, but by 10:00 am, we had polished off the champagne, and Ryley had totaled the breakfast spread. There was nothing left for us to do but get dressed and face our day.

We had agreed over breakfast that we would need to return to New Jersey, but I wanted to go immediately, and Ryley wanted to go in the evening. Of course, Ryley won that argument. There is no dragging a recalcitrant god somewhere he doesn't want to go.

I left my luggage in the room, taking only my oversized travel purse, which still had plenty of spell components left. Ryley left instructions at the desk that our suite should be cleaned and a late supper prepared and left for us tonight. I thought he was being optimistic, as I really wasn't expecting to survive the night, but he insisted.

It was a beautiful morning, with just a hint of late spring

crispness in the air. We walked up Fifth Avenue, window shopping. We started to pass a world-famous jeweler's store when Ryley made a surprise detour inside. There was a small showroom to our right and a second, grander door to our left. Instead of glass, it was a dark wood door with what appeared to be precious metal inlays. It was a work of art and clearly meant to dissuade the general public from that part of the jeweler's business.

Take a picture in front of the door, post it to Instagram, and move on was the message conveyed. Never one to take a hint, Ryley headed for that door, pulling me along as my arm was linked in his.

As soon as our intention to bypass the public access was clear, we were immediately greeted by the man apparently in charge of the exclusive entrance. Dressed in a crisp uniform complete with cap, the jeweler's doorman stepped forward.

That doorman was to be the first in the store to fall to Ryley.

As Ryley steered us toward the doorway, the doorman, just doing his job, politely and professionally blocked our way.

"Do you have an appointment, sir?"

"An appointment?" Ryley pulled to a sudden stop, unaccustomed to having to explain himself.

"To shop this morning," the doorman replied smoothly. "If you would let me know your appointment time and with which jeweler you will be consulting, I would be glad to escort you." He smiled, that efficient and non-threatening smile that he probably had to deploy dozens of times each day.

I felt Ryley's muscles tense, like a cat readying to play with a mouse.

"And if I don't have an appointment?" Ryley smiled back at the man, but it was a much more feral gesture, a showing of teeth rather than a friendly display.

"You are more than welcome to browse our showroom," and he gestured toward the public entrance, "or I would be glad to take you to someone who could make an appointment for you."

"I believe the lady and I will see someone without an appointment."

"I'm sorry, sir, but that is not possible at this time. As I said, I would be glad to have you speak to someone about setting a time and a jeweler to work with you."

Ryley tilted his head, assessing the man. His eyes bore into those of his prey. Ryley concentrated, wrestling with the doorman's will.

I watched, fascinated, as the man, at first nonplussed by our interaction, began to crack.

First, there was a twitch in his jaw. Then his eyes began to roll, unable to focus on us or on his task at hand.

"I can get you...a jeweler..." His tongue lolled out of his mouth as he was reduced to a broken vessel in a crisp uniform.

"Serve me." Ryley's deep timbre was quiet but commanding.

"Ia, ia, my lord." The doorman dropped to his knees and fell forward. He was practically salivating on Ryley's shoes. I could hear him whimpering faintly.

"Get up."

The doorman scrambled to his feet.

A crisp, "Allow us in," was all it took for the now slack-jawed man to obey.

It took a few tries for the doorman to put a code into a keypad I hadn't noticed, hidden as it was in a recess next to the door. When he was finally successful, the door clicked, and he pulled it open wide, bowing and gesturing for us to enter. He remained at the threshold, obviously in awe of his new god walking past him.

Once inside, we were swiftly escorted to a private shopping space. At first, the room looked like it could have been any conventional jewelry store showroom, save having it all to ourselves and the panoramic view of Fifth Avenue out the front windows. We were repeatedly assured that every piece on display was an original, not for standard public offer. Large diamonds, rubies, emeralds, and sapphires winked from settings ranging from simple to ostentatious. Necklaces, earrings, and rings adorned every display case. I wouldn't have been surprised if each piece had its own insurance rider. The collective worth of the room boggled me, although I tried hard not to show it. An assistant brought Ryley and I some refreshments for our shopping excursion, so we were enjoying a glass of sparkling wine as we looked.

In truth, I had no idea why we were here. This was all Ryley's doing. I was just enjoying seeing pieces of jewelry that would be more at home on the neck of an ingenue at a red carpet event than they would be in everyday wear.

After browsing aimlessly for a few minutes, the clerk trailing behind us obsequiously, Ryley announced he liked precisely none of the offerings and asked the man for a selection of aquamarine rings. He also specified that he wanted opals with them.

"Are you sure you want that particular stone, sir? The aquamarine is certainly an attractive stone, but it's only a semi-precious gem. Its cousin in beryl, the emerald, is quite stunning if you'd like to see..."

"Aquamarines and opals. Now."

A professional to his core, the man didn't hesitate a second time. He scurried from the room, leaving us on our own, which had to be a breach in their security procedures.

Ryley set down his empty glass on the counter and patted my hand, still tucked into his arm. He smiled, and I felt my stomach flutter at the tender gesture.

"I didn't forget your birthstone, Morningstar. An October baby. I remember how you love opals."

It wasn't long before the man returned with a custom tray of wares. He led us to a proper counter and smoothly moved behind it. The tray held several rings. Some were plain settings with different cuts of aquamarine. A few were opals, many of which the salesman said were from Coober Pedy, including an incredible black opal surrounded by diamonds. "See anything you like, sir?" he asked, gesturing to the tray.

Knowing better than to balk at one of Ryley's "gifts," I looked over the selection. Every one of them was gorgeous and show-stopping in its own right; however, only one ring on the tray included both stones. I could tell he noted when it caught my eye. I didn't say a word, but he pointed right to it.

"We need that one," he said.

"Excellent choice, sir," the man said as he handed Ryley the ring. "This is a two-carat trilliant cut aquamarine, flanked by cabochon cut fire opals in a platinum setting." He appeared to be holding his breath as Ryley slipped it on my left ring finger.

He exhaled when he saw it was a perfect fit.

The ring sparkled under the store lights, but it positively dazzled as I took it to the window, and sunlight hit it. Although it paled in a price comparison to the other wares we were shown, it was everything I didn't know I wanted.

"Aquamarine for me, and opal for you. Brilliant. The perfect fit. Just like the two of us together."

Impulsively, I kissed Ryley.

"We'll take it," he said.

"Will the lady be needing the ring box?"

"No, I'll just wear it out. Thank you."

"I can write that up for you and…"

"No need," Ryley cut him off. That voice again. Ryley's resolve made aural. I could see him forcing his will on the man a little harder, leaning on him in a metaphysical way. "We're just leaving with it. No box. No bill."

I saw the man's mental shift, the exact moment he lost his battle for his own free will. Lost himself and everything he ever was, at least for the moment. His shoulders slumped a little, his posture relaxing with his defeat. Most of our transactions had been conducted in relatively good faith until it was no longer convenient for Ryley to play human. Up until now, he'd been practically toying with the man, but he broke him.

Ryley broke him because he could. Because he enjoyed it. Because he was Ryley, the human form of an all-too inhuman, malevolent god.

It occurred to me that Ryley was leaving a hell of a body count in his wake just in this one day, now that his mental powers seemed to be gaining. I suspected it was proximity to his powers, tucked away in my little nautilus. So many people hurt, some irretrievably broken, just on a whim. People who didn't deserve this. People who would suffer because I called the evil into their midst.

Then I realized that way deep down - in a crevasse in my soul - I didn't like to admit even existed. I thought it was kind of sexy. Anything I wanted, anytime I wanted it. No more than a thought need be expended for all I desired to fall into my hands. I looked at the ring; then I looked at Ryley, as he leaned harder on the man.

The man blinked heavily a couple of times then nodded.

"Ia ia, my lord," the clerk said, the professionalism instilled in him to the bone, but with a dazed look in his eye now. He wouldn't remember us by the time the police came if he even called them, and cameras rarely captured anything close to Ryley's image. He was a digital ghost from a pre-analog time.

"Call us the elevator."

"Very good." The man shuffled to the elevator and pushed the button as Ryley and I walked over to him. He just stood there, looking at us but not seeing us. Again with the blank stare, awaiting any further orders.

Which is exactly where we left him. We retraced our steps, passing the folks who'd been in a holding pattern for the better part of an hour. The doorman quickly let us out, throwing himself on the floor behind us and sobbing, whether, in adoration or relief, I couldn't really say.

And just like that, we stepped back out onto Fifth Avenue and into the sunshine. Still holding on to Ryley, I had to shade my eyes from the blinding light with my other hand. Ryley reached into his jacket with his free hand and pulled out the sunglasses he'd acquired the day before. Whipping them on in one slick move, he moved forward without missing a step.

CHAPTER 8

A Little More Than 20 Years Ago

N early two dozen men in dark green robes formed a semi-circle before a stone gate. The gate, dredged from the bottom of the ocean off of Massachusetts under the cover of a marine archaeology expedition, appeared to be Ashford black marble or possibly obsidian, although, in reality, it was neither. To the casual observer, it appeared to be mostly black, but in bright light, such as a fully moonlit night like this, one could detect the dark green and catch hints of gold flecks deep in the stone.

The quarry from which the three pieces were procured was not of this planet and of no material known to man. Designs covered the ageless gate like profane graffiti, and although they had been etched into the surface, gouged nearly a half-inch deep, their smooth edges indicated this was not done by crude human hands. Glyphs imprinted into the gate included astral maps depicting constellations unknown to Earth-bound astronomers. A careful observer might also be disconcerted to see a map that appeared to be of the whole Earth itself, with a particular five-pointed sigil over a point that would correspond to the far South Pacific, near a place geographers named Point Nemo in the heart of the South Pacific Gyre. How this map of the Earth came to be on this wholly extraterrestrial and inexplicable ancient formation might have been greatly debated by scholars had the marine archaeology expedition been a legitimate academic exercise instead of a ruse.

However, as it had been plunder as part of a power play by a relatively small and obscure secret sect in Eastern New Jersey, the cosmic and cosmological implications of this information would never be debated in the Ivory Tower or, indeed, anywhere at all. Instead, these twenty-three men now ringed the front of the gate for the purpose of calling forth that which was on the Earth but not of it, that which was not dead but could eternal lie.

"Ia! Ia! Cthulhu fhtagn!" all the men would chant in unison.

"Ph'nglui mglw'nafh Cthulhu R'llyeh wgah'nagl fhtagn," the lone leader in the red robe would intone solemnly. The leader, Randall Laffite-Youx, expected complete obedience from his followers, and he received it in abundance.

"Ia ia, Cthulhu!" they would cry again.

This call and response went on as the full moon rose and beamed through the gate, bathing the men in a ghostly light. Their arms, wildly gesticulating as they chanted, made shadows on the beach, appearing as tentacles writhing on the sand before the gate.

"Ia! Ia! Cthulhu fhtagn!" rang out across the beach in waves of aural devotion.

Finally, Randall stepped before the gate. He pulled something out from within his robe and held it out toward the gate as his followers continued to chant. In his right hand, he held a small, deformed nautilus shell attached to what appeared to be a silver chain looped about his neck. As the cacophony reached its crescendo, the leader placed his left hand upon the gate itself, which sparked beneath his touch, and bellowed into the beyond, "Ia! Ia! Cthulhu! Cthulhu, ron sll'ha al shugg!"

A great roar emanated from the gate itself and from the other side. Viewed from the beach, nothing could be seen on the still waters of the surrounding ocean, but through the gate, the view was much different. The leader and his followers saw a roiling sea, myriad spouts of water nearly a mile high twisting on the horizon, and a great beast rising from the depths. A nightmare unleashed upon the world.

At first, only its hideous tentacles breached the water, but soon a vaguely humanoid form followed, monstrous in both size and appearance. It walked between the towering waterspouts, occasionally downing one with a massive swipe of its clawed hand. It tipped its head back and roared again, making clear from where the earlier noise had originated. Flexing its spike-tipped fingers and rolling its head on its shoulders, the creature's tentacles undulated in the night sky. Suckers opened and puckered, their moist cups reflecting the moonlight.

As the followers' chanting began to slow and trail off, possibly because their minds were breaking under the weight of the significance of the eldritch horror lurching toward them, their leader screamed over his shoulder, "More!"

When they mumbled and stumbled, he yelled, "Louder!" without ever breaking contact with the gate.

When their voices became discordant and panicked, he screamed, "Call him! Bring him to us! Ia! Ia! Cthulhu, ron sll'ha al shugg!"

Enough voices picked up the chant again to catch the creature's attention. Slowly the beast resumed its terrible lumbering toward the beach.

As it grew nearer to the gate, the shell in Randall's hand glowed a sickly green. Like a toxin emitted from within, it illuminated his right hand as well, making it appear as if the contamination were spreading through the man's very essence. This beacon called the beast ever closer.

"Yes," he whispered, "you will be mine. Come to me."

When the beast was so close to the other side of the gate that the stench of its foulness proceeded it, it finally realized that it was not going to fit through the mousehole of an opening offered to it. With another growl of frustration, the beast kicked at the gateway, sending a wall of water crashing through to the other side, soaking Randall and nearly knocking him off of his feet.

"Something is wrong!" Randall cried out. Looking frantically behind him, he saw that several of his fellows had either fainted or disappeared and at least two were stumbling in circles and screaming incoherently. His half circle was broken, and the glow of the shell began to fade.

"Jensen! Come to me," he called his second to his side.

Ever obedient, Jensen stepped up to the leader, agog at the swirling chaos he could see within the gate.

"My dagger. Pull it out."

The underling pulled a wicked-looking dagger from a sheath at his own waist. Jensen had been with Randall since they'd both fled New Orleans all those years ago, and he followed his leader unquestioningly. His recent promotion to Randall's second-in-command had been a dream come true for the aging cultist. To carry the ancient dagger was a blessing bestowed on only the most worthy. When the leader had asked *him* to hold the ceremonial dagger, *him* to protect it during the ceremony, Jensen had been all too willing to help. To be so close to power, you could taste it on your tongue. Exquisite!

He'd cradled that silver dagger in his hands, marveling at the hilt that looked like some terrible bird's talons. He had lovingly caressed the serpentine design on the handle. He had worn it all night at his waist to display to his fellows that he was Not A Man To Be Trifled With. Now, in the moment his leader needed him, he was all too eager to hold the dagger firmly, present for any part he might play in the ritual.

"We need blood on the gate. To call him through. Offer it yours. And we shall rule by his side for eternity. Now, Jensen, now!"

Ever obedient, without hesitation, Jensen ran the knife, swift and sure, across his left palm. He placed his palm against the gate, and it soaked up his offering like a sponge. In shock at the strange feeling, he recoiled. There was no blood to be seen where Jensen's hand had just been, not even a smear to recognize his sacrifice.

Randall observed the gate's reaction to Jensen's blood as well as its reaction when Jensen broke contact. It was what the gate wanted, but it hadn't been enough.

"More, Jensen. The gate needs more!" Randall shouted into the chaos.

Jensen slashed again with greater pressure, making a deeper parallel cut to the first. In his zealous enthusiasm to please Randall and to revisit that connected sensation with the gate, he forced the sharp edge farther into his hand than he should have. The greedy blade found its mark – slicing nerves, tendons, and muscles – severing his radial and ulnar arteries with one swift incision. Blood gushed from his hand. Jensen slapped his mangled palm back onto the gate, pressing it hard into the carved symbols.

The gate drank deeply.

Jensen could feel the stone sucking at the wound in a way that was both painful and erotic, draining him in every way he had to give. He moaned and braced himself with his other hand, which was still holding the dagger. Sparks flew from the point of contact between the metal and the gate, but Jensen was lost in an orgasmic connection to his god. This moment was everything he had always wanted in this life. A dark love he thought he'd never know.

Randall watched as Jensen moaned and writhed with one hand firmly connected to the gate. The second rush of power the blood provided seemed to be wearing thin. Determined to bring their god through this gate and harness the divine powers for himself, Randall leaned over and managed to pull the dagger from his second's hand. Jensen, oblivious to everything but what he was feeling in the moment, ignored Randall and pressed himself into the gate fully, embracing it like a lover.

Randall took his chance to strike.

Randall slit Jensen's neck with such violence, he half decapitated the man, dagger biting into bone. Caught up in the sanguineous moment, the murderous cult leader relished the arterial spray dousing both him and the gate. It wasn't his first murder, but it certainly was the most satisfying to date. He took a moment to savor the coppery wetness he licked from his own lips. He watched the gate absorb all that was once Jensen – physically, mentally, and spiritually.

For Jensen, brief moments lasted a lifetime as he contemplated the power and the glory that would be his. He never felt the fatal cut administered by his trusted leader, only the completion of his connection to the gate. The ecstasy engulfed him, devoured him whole. He stood smiling for a moment, gouts of blood raining from his neck, every droplet eagerly soaked up by the stone. He turned to Randall, tried to say "thank you," though the only sound he made was a gurgle, then he pitched forward toward the opening of the gate.

Randall's pleasure in the violence was cut short when he realized that the man's body would break the plane between the two worlds before Cthulhu himself would. What this might do to the spell they were performing, he didn't know.

"No, Jensen! Not there!" he cried out.

But the deed was done.

Jensen's torso was no longer visible, but his legs stuck out from the arch, splayed apart on the sand. His body, a conduit between two worlds, shorting out the connection by crossing the wires. The light of the nautilus shell dimmed as it appeared to drain into the stone of the gateway, causing the stone to pulse with Jensen's heartbeat. The gate created a blinding green luminosity reflecting back onto the beach, fading slightly with each throbbing flash as Jensen's life ebbed out of him in another dimension beyond the gate.

A whooshing sound accompanied a massive suctioning of air and water through the gate and onto the beach. Randall was blasted from his position. His body rolled helplessly in the smallest, most focused tsunami to ever exist. He barreled into the remaining followers who had valiantly attempted to keep up the chant through the chaos. The waters churned viridescent, irradiated by the glow of the gate.

When the wave broke on the beach, and the water receded into the ocean, the view from within the gate and from the rest of the beach was once again the same. Cultists littered the beach, although many seemed physically unharmed as the men shook themselves and the sand from their robes while staggering to their feet. Only a few remained unmoving, bodies face down in the surf, seaweed trailing gently from their limbs with each small wave like swaying branches of a dead tree.

And there, in front of the now inert gate, was a gelatinous form pulsing with stolen life. And malice. It looked vaguely humanoid with tentacles protruding from its head. Each tentacle writhed with the rhythm of the waves on the beach. Each suction cup opened and closed like the mouth of a gasping fish. Two oversized, glassy eyes, reddish in color with black, rectangular pupils rimmed in gold, bulged from either side of the head. The cultists watched in abject horror as those eyes inexorably migrated forward on the creature, ostensibly offering it the binocular vision required for top predators. For one brief and terrible instant, the creature blinked and stole a baleful glance at the ragged assemblage before it.

In that moment, three of the men fell to the sand, screaming in agony and frothing at the mouth. Seafoam fell from their lips until they choked on it, then it spurted out their noses until they respired it. The other cultists gave those first direct victims barely any notice as the damned souls flailed and eventually expired on the beach, the foam and their breathing ceasing entirely.

As the creature pulled itself from the sand to stand, it continued to morph, taking on the shape of those around it. It pulled its tentacles into itself, changing them to long, curly, dark locks of hair. Claws reverted to hands and fingers, feet and toes. Its musculature, originally bulky and thick, both stretched and relaxed into a more sinewy form. Its skin morphed from a mottled greenish-black to an even golden bronze. Its face became a mélange of features that betrayed no trace of national or ethnic origin. Its eyes – those huge, red orbs – grew smaller and lighter, settling on a startling shade of aquamarine, their pupils rounded out and turned a black of unfathomable depth. It drew itself to a respectable height and squared off with its observers. When it finally stood erect before the cultists, its form was that of a man. Uncommonly handsome and statuesque, but just a man all the same.

And he was naked.

"Y'chtenff lw'nafh ilyaa, Cthulhu."

"Mnahn' Cthulhunyth, ya nog," the naked man replied. "Ya ch'nog R'lyeh."

Although Randall had some command of the tongue, he was unable to process the conversation properly and was concerned he would miss important nuances should they continue to converse in R'lyehian. He had one chance to get this right.

"Can you speak in English?"

The naked man worked his tongue in his mouth for a moment and said, "I can speak in all languages." His voice sounded harsh, guttural. "More languages than you can dream, ape."

Randall bristled. He was accustomed to unswerving obedience and ingrained servitude from his lessers. Of course, their god would be different, but he had at least expected to be treated as an equal, as he himself had brought Cthulhu out of his deep slumber.

Of course, he also knew anything less than unfailing politeness could result in his immediate termination from his position as well as his mortal coil.

"Of course, my lord Cthulhu. I meant no offense. We brought you here to rule with me over the Earth. As a haruspex of great renown, each day, I consulted the viscera for a sign of you."

Although the avatar before him would not know it, the leader spoke with just a hint of a Southern drawl, out of place in this odd East Coast setting. The slightly elongated and lower "a" and "o" sounds of the distant bayou were often mistaken for a Bostonian accent by those with whom the leader had to speak. Today, however, the leader's only linguistic goal was communicating with his god and keeping his own life while advancing his nefarious ambitions.

"Only this afternoon did I decipher the connection between our realms," the leader continued. "It augured well for your entry to our world. We just hadn't expected that you would be... so...human."

"Obviously, you have failed me." He pointed to the shell still dangling from the leader's neck, recognizing the vital component to a holding spell. "Give me my power."

Randall, with shaky hands, removed the chain from around his neck and handed it to his lord.

"When this is done, I shall wipe you and your wretched kin from this beach, from this shore, from this world!"

Cthulhu ripped it from his hands and began a chant on his

own, his voice smoothing into a more pleasant timbre with every word spoken.

"Y'gotha wgah'n ah ilyaa n'ghft uaah!"

As he spoke his power back into existence, he saw that exactly nothing happened. Like any frustrated person, he gave the shell a few shakes and tried again, repeating the incantation more forcefully.

Still nothing.

"It is not working!" he roared in indignation. Looking up, he caught the glow of the archway next to which they stood. "My power is in the stones. Place your hands on the stone and transfer to me my power."

Randall, while not necessarily the smartest man in New Jersey, was certainly getting the idea that this entire encounter was turning against him apace. If he was right about what happened, he had a way out. If he was wrong, he would be dead before his body hit the sand. He had one play left, and it had to be perfect.

"No, my lord."

With a glare that tolerated no insubordination, he growled, "What did you say to me?"

"I said, no." He motioned to his stunned followers. "Seize him."

Cthulhu moved forward in a rush, right arm extended, apparently planning to get the leader by the throat. Instead, he found himself with an odd sensation in his torso. Halting his charge, he looked down to see the leader holding a dagger to his middle, with just the tip of the metal piercing his skin. A trickle of red ran down from the point of contact.

Very human blood.

"You need someone to give you your power voluntarily, and I do not volunteer. Not again."

Randall's followers, seemingly jolted back to their duties by the sight of blood seeping from their god, returned to executing their leaders' wishes. Two of the larger followers jumped in, and each forcefully took an arm of their fallen deity.

"Release me." Cthulhu looked the leader straight in the eye. "I command you," he intoned heavily.

"Yeah, that's not really going to work on me." The leader managed a crooked half-smile. "Won't work on my men either. We're already broken, Great One. Pacts with elder gods? Reading the stars in the night sky, even ones that aren't there? Studying books in long dead alien languages about worlds never imagined by men? We've done it all and more. In pursuit of knowledge. In pursuit of power."

He lowered his dagger, still clutched tightly in his right hand, and poked at Cthulhu's chest with the index finger of his left hand. "In pursuit of you. The biggest disappointment of all."

Cthulhu struggled against the hands that held him fast.

"You're pathetic. All this time, waiting, sacrifice... and for what? You're nearly powerless. Your mental powers are but parlor tricks to us."

By now, Randall was preening, lecturing his god as one would a wayward child. Putting on a demonstration for his followers.

"But I will have your power still. Because it is here," he pointed to the archway. "Locked away until the stars align again. By that time, I will figure out how to transfer that power to me. I will become the god I seek, and you will be but a pet on my chain."

Aquamarine eyes bore into him with the force of death itself, and Randall gave it no mind. His soliloquy finally neared its conclusion. He'd been pacing back and forth, intermittently jabbing a finger into the chest of his prisoner, but now his pacing ceased. He squared off with the newly made man, still struggling in the clutches of Randall's followers.

"Take him to the cell in the basement. Give him a robe but no sash, no shoes. Wouldn't want any accidents, would we? I don't yet know if he can slip back to R'lyeh if he dies in this form or if he can die at all. But I need him alive. Alive and under my complete control."

He waved his hand dismissively, turning away from his prisoner. "Be gone."

Wordlessly, Randall gazed at the ocean through the portal. He heard the loud protestations of his prisoner as the man was dragged away, expressing profanities and extreme violence in at least four languages, one of which had likely never before been heard on Earth. Randall felt the weight of a dozen stares at his back as he contemplated this setback for his organization. He had to take immediate and ruthless control of the situation.

His specialty.

He turned around to address his expectant flock.

"This is a glorious day for us, Brothers! Our god has come forth, as we bade him to do, and he has placed his power with us, for safekeeping, in our gate." He gestured to the archway with a grand flourish. "Jensen has already ascended to await us. For now, we must play host to our god's frail human form. We must guard him carefully and prepare for the coming time when we rule the world. The stars will realign, and our demands will not be denied!"

There were nods and murmurs of agreement from the remaining cultists. When the leader knew his position was secure, and the men would follow him unquestioningly again, he continued. "Take our fallen brothers to the house to be given proper tribute and preparation for their journeys in the Aether. Then prepare yourselves for the coming time of sacrifice and glory as new gods upon this Earth."

CHAPTER 9

I was enjoying our stroll and admiring my new ring, but I knew we still had one major hurdle. That was finding a way to New Jersey.

Although I loved taking trains anywhere, Ryley detested any form of public transportation. He needed things to run on his schedule completely at his convenience. He needed to be in control at all times. That ruled out planes, trains, and taxis. It was even difficult to get him to consider hiring a private car because it meant he wasn't driving.

Ryley was the very definition of the phrase "control freak." But then again, when one was a god...

"What about a boat, Morningstar? We could take a leisurely cruise to New Jersey."

"You gonna hijack the Staten Island Ferry, or did you have something else equally inconspicuous in mind?"

He made a little pout because he didn't like me making fun of him, but he must have been in rare high spirits to let my comment slide without a rejoinder.

We walked a little further in silence, soaking up the atmosphere of a sunny and unseasonably warm day. If it wasn't for the occasional odd stares as people passed us, it would have been absolutely normal. They must have sensed that something was incredibly wrong in their world for just that moment, like that chill that tells you Death was nigh but not coming for you. At least not today. If it wasn't for the fact that we were actually plotting an event that could result in my untimely death or the end of the world, we could have maybe passed for young lovers enjoying the Big Apple. Well, he would be the young lover. I guess I would be the late September to his early May in the time-worn cliché of romance. Seeing the looks and thinking about our history kind of put a damper on my mood, so I set that all aside to enjoy the moment.

Sunshine. A gorgeous ring. Ryley, warm and human, next to me.

We did what any other couple might do on such a beautiful day. We window shopped, although we had no need of anything else. We stopped at the random food cart for a pretzel or a bag of warm sugared almonds. I paid for the treats to keep Ryley from leaning on the vendors too hard. I wanted to keep up the charade of normalcy, just for myself, even if I knew it was all lies and self-serving delusions. As we meandered along, Ryley pulled us a few blocks off of Fifth Avenue to stop for a late lunch at one of his favorite restaurants. Although it was a nondescript, hole-in-the-wall kind of place, Ryley had brought me here many times during our senior year of college. He said he'd found it when he first hit New York, and he'd been a regular ever since.

Of course, now I wondered when exactly that was – his first time in the city. I also wondered if we would ever get a chance to have that conversation. Time was running out for me. The window of opportunity to have my many questions answered was closing rapidly. I also worried what the answers might mean for my immediate future, leaving me too afraid to ask.

But for now, I could take pleasure in what used to be our routine as we approached the door, the lettering a little more scratched and worn with age but the neon "Open" sign still flickering a bright red. I could tell he was looking forward to eating here again by the way he quickened his steps and mine as we got closer. He seemed to enjoy the atmosphere, and he really savored the food. What was most unusual was that Ryley always paid in full when we ate there. I remember he always made a show of taking care of the bill at this restaurant, although I could never remember him paying a single tab anywhere else. That was a sign of respect that the owners would likely never know had been accorded to them.

When we walked in, I was assaulted by a thousand memories of this place. The smell of the grease from the kitchen hung in the air, perfumed with spices and whiffs of their specialty dishes. It brought back the late-night munchie runs when we'd been the only people left in the place, happily slurping our soups and giggling like mad over some joke or stolen moment. I remembered one early morning staggering in here after all night at the bars and clubs, when we almost passed out in our lo mein and took boxes of the stuff back home, only to fall into bed together at his apartment and sleep until the late afternoon. So many of my best memories of Ryley took place here. I'd never been able to return without him.

I couldn't. It would just be another aching reminder of how lonely I'd been for so many years.

We walked in just ahead of the lunch rush, so there were only a few other patrons when we arrived. As I stood, looking at the faded travel posters for Chinese cities and sites, remembering their original colors from what seemed so long ago, Ryley made his wishes clear to the staff. The hostess seated us at a larger table with a slightly chipped glass top. She appeared flustered when he demanded to be seated at "his" table, which clearly was designed for at least a dozen people, but she did it without complaint. She left us each with a menu and headed to the kitchen, probably to ask her management about the couple taking up a banquet table.

This brought out the owners. The same folks we'd known from years ago. I was amazed that they were still here, still running the place. They had been impossibly old fifteen years ago, but they looked much the same today when they came to our table to greet us. I could see their surprise when they stepped into the dining room.

"Mr. Ryley and Miss Amanda! It's been so long!" the elderly man said as he approached our table. He walked with a pronounced limp now and was maybe a little more stooped but didn't appear much different otherwise. His wife kept pace with him and stood silently by his side, apparently sizing us up after such a long absence. "So good to have you back."

I smiled, remembering all the times we'd been here before, usually late into the evening, just as they were getting ready to close. But they always stayed open for Ryley. And he, in turn, always made it worth their while, showering the wait staff with praise and cash when paying our bill. It was a very un-Ryley thing to do, which I hadn't really noticed at the time when I was young and so in love. I was just ashamed I couldn't remember their names. Ryley probably never knew them. He didn't remember details about the lives of humans.

Except me. He always made me feel special.

"I was back in the city for the day and couldn't resist stopping for the best food in town," he said with a smile and a little wink for the missus. He was being especially gregarious and had sprawled himself in his little chair in that way he had of taking up as much physical space as possible. I could tell he was comfortable back in one of his old haunts.

The old man squinted hard at each of us then looked outside the tiny front window. "It's a little earlier than your usual table time."

I noticed that the old woman kept looking at me. She wasn't casual about it either. She was definitely scrutinizing us both, but I was getting the extra eyeball. Her eyes landed on my ring early in her assessment. I flashed it a little to make sure she got a good look. I wondered if she was jealous. After all, both Ryley and the ring were gorgeous. I could only imagine her thought process when the young couple she once knew no longer appeared to be the same age. Although I don't think of myself as looking "old," I did age in the fifteen years Ryley was away. I'd found a stray grey hair over the years. Still, I admit I felt a little bristly about the extra inspection. Ryley, of course, was oblivious.

"Unfortunately, we have an appointment this evening, so there's only time for lunch, but we'll have the usual if you please, Mr. Wang."

You could've knocked me back with a tap. Ryley remembered his name. That was unusual.

What wasn't unusual was that it never crossed Ryley's mind that the owner wouldn't remember his regular order from fifteen years ago, and apparently, there was no need to consider it. Mr. and Mrs. Wang must have had exceptional memories. Within minutes, appetizers began arriving at our table. Plates of wontons and dumplings borne by two young servers came first, followed by four different soups, including a bowl of their house special Roast Duck Wonton, all of which Ryley eagerly consumed. I managed a few wontons and my own bowl of egg drop soup. Ryley got everything else in the first round.

We were sipping green tea when the next course began. The two servers, at the direction of the owners and one cook, brought out several plates of their family-style meals. Ryley's "usual" wasn't really a particular dish so much as a buffet for one, which I was allowed to sample. They brought out more than a dozen options for us: four types of lo mein, moo shu plates, a whole pile of eggrolls, egg foo young, two versions of fried rice, a spicy noodle dish loaded with dried peppers, a plate of steamed buns, roast pork, and roast duck. The only thing Ryley didn't eat was seafood, and there wasn't a bite of it on the table. The old man remembered.

There was also only one standard plate, which was laid at my place. Another Ryley trait – family-style didn't exactly make for sharing at Ryley's table. He ate his pleasure. You took your chances as dishes moved past you.

I managed to put together a very nice plate of food, with a little bit from each plate. I enjoyed it tremendously for most of our meal, while Ryley tackled everything else with gustatory abandon. Although Ryley was usually less about talking and more about eating when it came to mealtime, today, he slowed down enough to discuss strategy as he polished off plate after plate.

"You're sure that we have to be back to the gate today?"

"Absolutely," I said between bites of chicken lo mein. I was confident, having meticulously researched this for years. "Everything I've read in my research leads to this exact time. It's wild. Texts from ancient sources cite this modern date. And then there's Trekkie. The light of those stars is coming from somewhere, and I think the final pieces will pop into place tonight. We have to be there. It's imperative."

Ryley finished his plate and set it on a stack of empty plates to his right, pulling in another full platter in one smooth motion.

"If you would just let me acquire us a car, we can be on our way."

"Fine," I acquiesced with little grace. He'd been suggesting this solution for the last several blocks of our walk, but I hadn't wanted to take that option. "Steal a car and drive us there, but then we don't really get to spend any more quality time with each other."

"We'll have plenty of time together when the ritual is done, Morningstar. We will have eternity." He smiled at me with his mouth, but his eyes were intense, their shade darkening a little like a storm blowing in from the sea. This was a predator nearing the end of a long hunt, finally circling his prey and ready for the take down. He'd been planning this power move since before I was born, probably before all of humanity. He was finally seeing the culmination of millennia's worth of strategy, just to bet it all on the magic of a single human.

And he was excited about it.

I should have been afraid, I realized, being that single human, but I just couldn't work up the terror. Everything about our situation was a dichotomy. I was having a leisurely lunch with the love of my life, who truly was evil incarnate. The most beautiful man I'd ever seen was here with me, but he wasn't a man at all. He was talking about spending forever together, but I was plotting a scheme that would result in the demise of one of us. Or maybe both of us. One slip of the tongue could change who survived and who sunk to an underwater oblivion. With all the conflicting thoughts running rampant in my head, there was no room for fear.

He patted my hand in a gesture I assumed was meant to be reassuring and resumed his feast. I, on the other hand, pushed away my plate and contemplated the next 12 hours of my life, which could easily be my last. For the last few years, I'd been planning this down to every minute detail – calling Ryley, getting back to Novastella Manor, heading down to the beach, reciting the spell that would send us through the gate – possibly to my death, possibly a worse fate – not even knowing how that would affect the rest of the world. But now that it was all coming together, I had to wonder if I was doing the right thing. Was this really the way I wanted everything to end? Did it really have to be now? I slowly rubbed my nautilus shell back and forth between the fingers and thumb of my right hand. The clock was ticking down, and I still wasn't completely sure what I was going to do when the time came.

I could only manage a few nibbles when they brought dessert, having most of an almond cookie and half of a fortune cookie. Ryley devoured the remainders of the one dozen of each type of cookie. Plastic wrappers and the tiny paper fortunes lay scattered across his placemat, unread and disregarded. He always found it annoying that they put paper in his dessert.

I used to find it interesting, and kind of funny, that every fortune Ryley ever got was blank. Every single one.

Today, mine was blank too.

Now it didn't feel quite so entertaining. Bad omen or a sign of my upcoming success? Maybe I wasn't cut out for this Machiavellian shit. I just didn't know.

As I stewed over my own cosmic existential crisis, the server approached our table daintily and tried to unobtrusively slide the bill under a plate near Ryley's arm. We'd been sitting at her table for nearly three hours, enjoying the food and our conversation, but the dinner crowd would be coming soon. Once the tab hit the table, she scurried away like a frightened rabbit. Whether it was to avoid interrupting us or fear of the reaction at the amount, I didn't know, and, in that moment, I didn't really care. I was starting to feel suffocated by this fake normalcy of our late lunch date, and I wanted to get on with it, whatever "it" turned out to be.

Either not aware or not caring about my spiraling mood, Ryley downed the last of his tea and picked up the check from the table.

"Ready, Morningstar?" He reached his hand out to me.

"Sure, Ry." I slid my hand into his and let myself revel again in the feeling of his warm skin. Torn between what I thought I wanted and what I needed, I looked him straight in the eye and smiled. "I'll go anywhere with you."

He smiled back. We walked up to the cash register. I was surprised to see Mr. Wang waiting there instead of the hostess.

Ryley set the bill on the counter and gestured over it with his hand. "Would you be so kind as to take care of this?"

So apparently, Ryley wasn't in a bill-paying mood today.

Mr. Wang smiled, his eyes crinkling at the edges as if Ryley had just told the most amusing joke. I was expecting to turn and leave, as we always did in this situation, when Mr. Wang placed one slim finger onto the bill, tapping it twice.

"No, Mr. Ryley. You know the rules here." He kept his gaze steady on Ryley.

I could feel the tension in the air as Ryley and Mr. Wang engaged in some sort of battle of wills. I'd never seen anything like it. It's hard to explain, but there was almost a *violence* simmering beneath the exchange, although neither of them made a move toward the other.

It was Ryley who broke first.

He laughed and reached into his front pocket to retrieve the wad of cash he'd taken from the young man yesterday on the docks. Peeling off five of the one-hundred-dollar bills, he tossed them lightly onto the counter.

"Will this be sufficient, Mr. Wang?"

Mr. Wang picked up the bills and glanced at our check.

"Always a pleasure having you here, Mr. Ryley. Do come back again the next time you return to the city." The old man briefly smiled at Ryley, then he nodded to me. "Good luck, Miss Amanda."

He turned away first, returning to the back of the restaurant, while I was left wondering what exactly he meant. Before I had time to consider it further, Ryley put my hand on his arm and went to the front of the restaurant. He opened the door for me and gestured outside.

"Lead the way," he said, bowing slightly in a mock display of chivalry.

We walked hand-in-hand back to Fifth Avenue and began our search for mutually agreed-upon transportation.

By now, the Friday afternoon foot traffic had picked up considerably. We shared the sidewalk with throngs of tourists as we inched closer to a favorite shopping area. Ryley bristled as he was forced shoulder-to-shoulder with the masses, as I had asked him to dampen his usual talent for creating a circle of space around us. I wanted to get back to my happy place before I had to go to New Jersey, my anti-happy place. I had decided to go for normalcy and, today, at this moment, it meant being jammed onto the sidewalk with hundreds of other people.

At one point, it was so crowded, I found myself out ahead of Ryley, pulling him along in my wake. I laughed.

"Keep up, Pokey. Wouldn't want to lose you now!"

He dug in his heels and brought us both to a stop. In an instant, people flowed around us like water. He pulled me to him and kissed me. It was a fierce kiss, a possessive kiss.

"I will never lose you, Morningstar. I am drawn to you, to your every need and desire. I can feel them inside of me. I felt them beneath the waves as I feel them now. There is nowhere you could go that I wouldn't follow. You're irresistible to me."

He kissed me again with such passion that it took my breath away. He actually lifted me up to him, holding me tight against his body as his hands roamed over my back, cupping my ass to pull me more firmly against him. Forgetting for a moment that we were in public, I eagerly climbed him and returned his ardor. When he finally set me back down on the sidewalk, I was still reeling and aching from unfulfilled need. Slowly, the crowds closed in again, and we were just two people blocking the sidewalk.

CHAPTER 10

Two Years Ago

S *tellam Matutinam.*
        Amanda's mother had mumbled the strange phrase during one of her recent episodes. Caroline had said it clearly and in an unnatural voice. Amanda was pretty sure her mother had no idea what she was saying or any grasp of the significance of her words. Caroline had also chanted some strange phrases Amanda didn't recognize, so she wrote them down phonetically for future reference. Now her research into a whole list of phrases had led her to the restricted section of the basement of a small East Coast college that seemed to have more ivy-covered buildings than students on campus. It had become her go-to for all matters magical and occult when she began doing research on Ryley.
    Stellam Matutinam.
    That was the name of the spell. The magic spell would create a concubine for Cthulhu to lure him from his dark city beneath the waves. Amanda finally found it in a dusty forgotten book in

the same library she'd found all manner of strange tomes. This book was bound in light leather with silver fittings on the corners. At least, she hoped it was leather. She couldn't fathom why the library kept these strange books in their Restricted Collection, but she was grateful to have access to them.

According to the book, this spell could be used by a man to make the lure. She found herself disgusted at the details, which apparently involved a willing female vessel to incubate the lure. Once the creature entered the world, it could be used to entice Cthulhu, but its power increased with the time it spent synching itself with the planet. For the greatest chance at success, the spellcaster should plan two to three decades to allow the lure to mature.

As she took her notes, it occurred to her that the title was likely in Latin. She made a note to look up the name before she left the library. The one linguistics class she took in college was only minimally helpful to her in this situation. She could guess that the first word, *stellam*, probably shared the same root word as stellar, so it might mean star. It seemed like the cultists she'd researched were big into the idea of stars aligning, even more so than astrologists. The second word was a mystery to her, but she continued working.

Amanda took dutiful notes on the spell, including the components needed to gather the magic and the words needed to speak it into existence. She obviously didn't plan on replicating the spell any time soon (or ever), but information always made her feel better. "Forewarned is forearmed" had become her motto since that night she and Ryley went to New Jersey, and only she had returned. The cultists were dangerous, and any knowledge of their rituals and methods could make a difference for her someday.

Especially if I ever need Ryley. I might need that lure to bring him back.

She shook off that thought and finished her notes. She made

a side note to figure out how to find the lure, so she could retrieve it if necessary. But that information quest would have to wait for another day. Reading these books and transcribing the spells was mentally exhausting work. She could only manage to do one in a day, even if it only took a few hours. It was the reason she booked a week at her favorite hotel in the area every time she came to do research.

Amanda thanked the strange little man, Mr. Hereford, who always worked the Restricted Collection room. He never spoke to her, just nodded to indicate he'd heard. When she first started coming here, she thought maybe he was upset because she wasn't an academic. In fact, she had originally been denied access to these books precisely because she wasn't affiliated with any college or university. But like most colleges, a well-placed donation to the school's foundation opened doors. So she'd made one. A sizable donation, in fact. The president himself had extended his school's credentials to her, and she gained access to all of the academic resources any full professor there could use. She had been thrilled to discover that her access extended to several other small colleges and universities on the East Coast. A few more donations ensured the access was smooth and friendly for her at every library she wanted to visit.

Of course, just because she had credentials didn't mean she had acceptance by everyone. Money could buy access but not respect. After initially refusing her requests by email, by telephone, and in person, Mr. Hereford had simply nodded his acquiescence with a taut frown when she appeared at his desk six months ago with her paperwork in order. His last refusal had been the last words she'd heard out of his mouth. She still said hello and goodbye to him, in addition to letting him know her needs during any given visit.

It rankled Amanda that he treated her as less than. Had he met any dark gods? She didn't think so. And she was personally acquainted with one. She was not certain if his disdain for her was genuine or, at this point, just habit. She thought maybe it irritated him that she was always so chipper, and so she made a point to be as cheery, and even overly familiar, as possible whenever she interacted with him.

"Have a great night, Hereford. See you bright and early tomorrow," she practically chirped as she passed by his desk with a wave.

His stoic stare was all the reaction she expected for her gesture, but it made her smile. Torturing the stuffy archivist with excessive kindness always gave her a lift.

The librarians at the front were much friendlier, and Amanda always enjoyed talking with them. They were also used to her unusual requests and actually seemed to enjoy the research challenges she presented. Amanda swung by the Reference Desk on her way out and was greeted by the Reference librarian, who was at her usual post.

"Good afternoon, Ms. McDaniel." The librarian smiled. "How can I help you today?"

"Today is an easy one, Rhonda. I just need a translation of a Latin phrase, *Stellam Matutinam*."

"That shouldn't be too tough." Rhonda walked back into her reference area and pulled a Latin-English dictionary from a shelf. Returning to the desk, she opened the dictionary and started working through it. As the librarian worked her reference magic, Amanda looked around, leaning on the desk, admiring the 19th Century woodwork and copper-plated ceiling tiles. She loved this old library and its Ivory Tower ambiance.

"Okay, *stellam*, a form of *stella* or star."

"That's what I thought," Amanda interjected.

Rhonda spared a brief glance at her.

"Astronomy stuff from my previous, pre-author life," Amanda lied easily with a shrug, "but I have no idea about the second word."

"Alrighty then, *matutinam*." She flipped through the dictionary. "Let's see, feminine singular, adjective," she mumbled as she ran her finger through the entry. "Ah, morning or morrow. So, your phrase is the feminine for star of the morning or morning star. It could mean Venus or Lucifer, too. They are both referred to as morning star. I mean, that's literary or Biblical, respectively. Also, in astronomy, it could just be an antiquated way to refer to the planet, Venus. Heaven knows how old those books you study might be."

Rhonda looked up from the dictionary. "Are you okay, Ms. McDaniel? Do you need to sit down?"

Amanda felt like she'd been physically struck. The blood drained from her face, making her appear to be on the verge of fainting.

Stellam Matutinam. Morning Star. Her mind reeled.

"I thought it was a nickname because of the first time we met or my initials, for Amanda Melissa," she stammered. "Just a pet name. Between lovers." Her stomach lurched, and she unconsciously made a retching sound.

"What?" The concerned librarian started looking around for assistance like she was worried that this famous author was about to throw up on the desk or pass out on the floor.

"I'm...I'm sorry. I have to go. I have to get out. I just..."

Amanda put one hand over her own mouth. Whether to quell the retching or stifle a scream, she wasn't sure. She turned and headed for the front door without another word, leaving the very confused librarian calling behind her. She made a beeline for her car and got in, sitting down heavily, tossing her book bag on the passenger's seat beside her.

She couldn't wrap her mind around what she'd just learned. She started to hyperventilate. The interior of the car spun, and everything outside the car was a blur. Gathering her remaining wits, she tried to slow her breathing. Amanda inhaled through her nose and exhaled through her pursed lips, consciously focusing on each breath, so she wouldn't have to think about the implications of her findings.

In, out.

In, out.

Morning star.

Her chest tightened. *Breathe. C'mon, McDaniel, breathe!*

In, out.

In, out.

When she could finally breathe normally, she closed her eyes to center herself. When she felt steady, Amanda opened her eyes and reached for her book bag. She pulled out her notes and reread them.

Okay, so maybe she was the Morning Star. In reality, she had already been Cthulhu's concubine, hadn't she? She and Ryley practically spent every night at his apartment off-campus by the Spring semester of her senior year. They'd certainly had a relationship.

And sex.

Lots of it.

She sighed. Even in the trauma of her new discovery, she had to admit, she did miss Ryley, even knowing what he was and now knowing what she was. If she really was the Morning Star from this ritual, any love he may have felt for her could have been little more than a magic trick. She loved him, of that she was certain. Nothing had ever felt more real than the months she'd spent as Ryley's lover. But was that the result of being made for him, literally, or did they have something genuine? Amanda anguished, wondering if she'd ever know the truth of that.

What she could learn for certain were more details on this spell and the meanings of a few more phrases she wanted to check. She still had six days left in town. Tonight, she would rest and regroup. Tomorrow, she would head back into that library, apologize to Rhonda for her outburst or whatever that was and return to the archives for another go at those cursed books.

Which was exactly what Amanda did. After treating herself to a lovely seafood dinner from room service, she spent the evening in the hotel reading a good romance novel and heading to bed early. Even then, she slept fitfully. Her dreams were dark, but there was nothing in them she could pin down – not for her writing, not for her own peace of mind. Still, she had research to do. She put on just enough makeup to cover the dark circles beneath her eyes and stopped for a caramel latte with three extra shots of espresso on her way to the local touristy beach strip. She sipped, shopped, and strolled along the beach until she felt mostly herself again. Being close to the water always put her at ease and brought her a sense of connection to Ryley.

Another hour found her back in the library, true to her purpose.

She explained to Rhonda that she'd had a sudden onset of a migraine and apologized for her abrupt exit the day before. To amplify the apology, she brought Rhonda a box of chocolate truffles and a small bag of saltwater taffy from a famous, local boardwalk confectionery.

Amanda practically sang a bright good morning to Hereford as she breezed into the archives, handing him a list of books she wanted to see. She also set a single, gold-foil wrapped truffle on the counter, despite the strict rules forbidding food or drink in the Restricted Collection room. He scrutinized the treat for a moment, then set it daintily in a small paper bag he produced from behind the desk. He removed it to a spot Amanda couldn't see, then retrieved a little silver tea bell and its leather resting mat from behind the desk, placing it prominently before him and giving her a pointed look. He always set out his little bell, so Amanda could ring for him when he was in the back. He picked up her list and reviewed it. His scowl told her that everything was back to normal, or at least, that's how it appeared to others.

She took a seat at one of the four tables in the archives and waited for Hereford to deliver her a stack of books. While she waited, she pulled out a pair of white cotton gloves for handling the delicate tomes. She also set out her notebook and a few sharpened pencils, as no pens were allowed in the archives. Finally, she set a small cloth bag next to her notebook.

Early in her quest for information about Ryley, she'd learned to take precautions. Magical precautions. At first, she'd felt superstitious and foolish for trusting some bag of sand and herbs to somehow keep her safe from malevolent cosmic forces, but over time, she'd adjusted both the contents of the bag and her faith in it. When she hadn't seriously believed in the type of supernatural that she now knew to be both real and malevolent, she'd seen a manuscript that suggested using a personal bag of warding to protect the user from dark forces. On a lark, she'd sown a small bag from colorful tiki print material, left over from a piece of cloth she'd used for a craft project. Her bag sported bright red hibiscus flowers and tropical drinks with a sunny yellow drawstring tie. She added a few suggested "protective herbs," like hyssop and bay, and started carrying it with her when she researched. As Amanda's knowledge of the extensive cosmic horrors grew, she relied on that bag.

Now its festive appearance provided a startling contrast to its current fillings. These included dried seaweed and tiny shells from several beaches; the burned and ground bones of a strange fish she'd found offshore in Rhode Island; protective roots and herbs; and a small medallion inscribed with the Eye of Horus that was made from an unknown metal, which she'd purchased at a strange little shop in Salem the year before.

And Amanda was certain her eclectic little bag had spared her life – or at least her mind – on a few occasions.

In case Hereford was feeling feisty, she covered the bag with her archive gloves and waited for her first pile of books on the day.

He didn't disappoint. Fewer than 15 minutes later, Hereford reappeared with a small wooden trolley cart loaded with her requested tomes; then he disappeared into the back again. Amanda opened her notebook to the page of phrases she wanted to investigate. Her heart only stuttered a moment when she saw *Stellam Matutinam* in her own precise block writing again.

A lure for Cthulhu. A creature made to entice a dark god.

Me.

She shook her head and dove into her research. Amanda learned a long time ago that being studious and productive allowed her to push away any negative thoughts or worries, at least until a time when she could better process them. Right now, she was not quite ready to learn what it meant to be the lure. She did, however, find one passage that struck her as important. She copied it into her notes, word for word, as she would a spell or incantation.

And, lo, it is Prophesied! The Dread One, brought forth from his Eternal Slumber by the guiles of the Lure, shall lay low every man and beast – upon the lands and the seas – ushering in the Reign of Chaos!

So, *cross waking a dread god off the bucket list*, she thought, not that she had ever planned to do that in the first place.

Since she was seeking busy work today and not deep scholarship, she used her time to find out which tomes contained information on which phrases. She discovered that most of the phrases her mother uttered while in her weird fugue states were parts of magical incantations. The few that weren't must have been names of people or places, but they didn't appear to be directly connected to the rituals. In a rather nondescript tome on extraplanar objects and astronomy, Amanda noticed a newspaper article had been folded and tucked deep into the book. She was surprised that she even noticed it. The torn edges suggested haste, the yellowing copy suggested age, although there was no date on it. In the article, she found exactly one reference to "Laffite-Youx," which was on her list. There had been some sort of raid down in the bayous of Louisiana. The article stated that a bizarre death cult was broken up by the local authorities in a raid, resulting in the deaths or incarceration of most of the members. A few of their number apparently slipped away into the swamps, but the Laffite-Youx clan was considered to be extinct in the eyes of experts in such matters. She copied down the contents of the article word for word and tucked it back into the book. Content with what she considered a head start on the next day's research, she headed back to her hotel for a much deserved cocktail hour and a few laps in the pool.

Amanda returned to the Restricted Collection room every day for another week and a half, definitely overstaying her welcome with Hereford. Her searches during this research visit were quite fruitful. She left with a notebook full of incantations and gathered a great deal of the history of the Cthulhu cults. *Know thy enemy*, she thought, as she collected her notes on her last day. She was feeling good about this trip and her research, and she was looking forward to a final celebration dinner then a quiet evening in the hotel before she drove home in the morning.

As she left, she took a moment to stop and torture Hereford with some kindness. That always made her happy. As she stepped up to his desk to ring the little bell, she noticed something odd. The bell was in the same place as always, on a small, worn leather mat, but apparently, the last person to ring it had left the dainty bell turned 90 degrees. For the first time, she saw a symbol etched into the metal. It appeared to be a five-pointed star, but the lines of the star were a little wavy, and the star itself was misshapen as if someone had squished it down to one side. There were also lines in the center of it. She was pretty sure she'd seen it before in her readings.

Setting the bell down as softly as she could so it didn't signal Hereford, she took out her notebook and a pencil and sketched the symbol. She intended to go through her notes at a later time to figure out what it meant. While she drew, her eyes darted furtively to the door of the backroom. Amanda wasn't exactly sure why she didn't want Hereford to discover that she knew about the symbol, but she was pretty sure it might jeopardize her access, even with her donations to the college foundation.

When she finished her sketch, she put her notebook and pencil back into her bag, and she turned the symbol back to facing the person behind the desk. All of the mirth drained from her, Amanda left without even saying goodbye to her Restricted Collection nemesis. Instead, she practically snuck out the door and left the library without talking to anyone else.

CHAPTER 11

A s we moved down the crowded sidewalk once again, I saw that Ryley was scanning the street, leaving me to navigate us through the people. He was searching for our ride, our transportation to New Jersey. I compromised by agreeing he could steal a car. One last ride influenced by his whims and wants. After all, I had figured out that was how we got to Novastella Manor the first time. Why break a lucky streak?

Ryley didn't have any of the skills of a car thief. He couldn't hot wire a ride like some street tough in a movie. His skills were more of the persuasive kind. He needed to find a car that suited him with the driver still in the vicinity. Not having much luck in this section of Fifth Avenue, he was considering going back to our hotel to pick through whatever the valets had available. We hadn't walked too much farther when he pulled me to a halt. I stopped and looked up to see what apparently had his attention.

"That's it. Our ride." Ryley was smiling, which made me both a little excited and very nervous.

I followed his eyes and realized we were standing before St. Patrick's Cathedral. Its gothic grey spires stretched toward the blue sky as if its height alone could ascend its believers. There must have been a Friday early evening wedding because there were flowers set up in tiers up the massive steps up to the church and a beautiful, light tan vintage car parked on the curb.

"It's perfect!" he practically chirped as he began guiding, almost dragging, me through the crowd toward the car.

We crossed the street and made our way over. The back of the car had an old-fashioned steam trunk strapped to a small rear deck. It was a very squarish car, save for the dramatic curved fenders. Standing beside the car was a chauffeur decked out in 1930s period clothing, including a cap with driving goggles perched on top, a light tan duster that matched the car, and dark brown leather driving gloves. It had suicide doors, and the passenger side was open, revealing a cushy red velvet interior. Next to the door was a silver ice bucket on a stand. Chilling in the bucket was a green-necked bottle I was certain held champagne. As we approached, the chauffeur nodded politely to us, apparently thinking we were just tourists coming over for a gawk.

"She's a beauty," Ryley said, admiring the classic automobile.

"1934 Packard Straight-8 limousine, sir. Finest in her class, then and now."

Leaving me standing by the driver, Ryley walked around to the front, intently checking out the ornate headlights and the wheel-toting silver angel hood ornament.

"She's called the Goddess of Speed, an art deco masterpiece of design."

Ryley caressed her gently.

"I'm going to have to ask you to not touch the car, sir. The bride and groom will be out in an hour or so. I can give you a card if you and the lady are interested in renting it for an afternoon." The chauffeur looked at me and smiled. "Or for your own special occasion."

Ryley walked back around to us and looked directly into the

eyes of the driver. The intense leer causing the man's smile to falter and his legs to shake.

"Does she have a full tank of gas?"

"Yes, sssir," the man stammered, apparently falling quickly to Ryley's mental pressure.

"Is she roadworthy to get us to the northern shore of New Jersey, right now?" Ryley had stepped right into the man's personal space, aquamarine eyes boring into the poor soul.

"Ia, ia, my lord."

"Very good," Ryley said, a smile spreading across his face, lightening the mood for me. "The lady and I will be going to Highlands, New Jersey. Are you familiar with that town?"

The man nodded in the affirmative.

"I'll give you more explicit directions once we get there. And drive safely. We're the most important passengers you've ever had."

The man nodded again and moved to hold the door for us.

Leaving me beside the car, Ryley took a moment to walk over to the steps. I turned to watch him, half wondering who else he would require to do his bidding for our journey. Instead, he picked a few white roses from one of the sprays before returning to the car. Before entering, he grabbed the bottle from the ice bucket.

"Dom Perignon, how thoughtful. A wine knife?"

The driver reached into his pocket and pulled out an ivory-handled waiter's corkscrew. Ryley took it, snapped open the short knife blade on it, cut the foil, closed the blade, and tossed it onto the floor of the car.

He uncaged the cork and popped it with one hand, getting only a small pop from the bottle, then gestured for me to get into the car. I did, skootching across the seat and setting my purse on the floor by the opposite door.

Once I was seated on the cushioned bench, Ryley handed me the flowers and followed me inside, still clutching the champagne bottle. A small polished mahogany box on the floor opened to display two champagne flutes and a place to hold a bottle. I retrieved the glasses while our driver closed the door and went around to the other side.

There was a partition between us and the driver, although part of it slid to the side to allow for communication. Ryley closed it, having given the man his orders and knowing they would be followed exactly.

In a few moments, the driver was pulling onto the street, carefully and smoothly so as to not disturb our pouring. I kicked off my shoes, tucking them to the side by my purse, so I could curl my legs beneath me. Ryley did likewise with his shoes and hitched up one knee so he could face me.

After we settled onto the plush rear seat, Ryley poured our Dom. He set the bottle into the box and turned back to me.

"You wanted some privacy. See? I am capable of compromise."

"I suppose you are," I said, smiling at him. He'd still technically stolen the car, but he wasn't driving it. And I did have to admit, this was better than switching trains and taking taxis.

"A toast," he said, lifting his glass. "To us. To our past successes. And to our future."

We clinked glasses and sipped. It took me a moment to process his salute.

"What past successes?" I asked, enjoying the bubbly feeling tickling my nose. "Our last trip to New Jersey didn't really go so well. It was pretty much the opposite of a success, which is why we are going back to fix it."

"I meant your writing career, of course. I never thought you would actually make a go of things, considering how much you used to complain about how difficult the publishing industry is. But look at you! We did it."

The champagne soured on my tongue.

"*We* didn't do anything," I said, trying to reign in my anger.

"*I* worked my ass off, writing day and night, submitting every-thing I could. We aren't an author. I am."

Ryley's eyes narrowed, and I could see the fight looming. Both my timing and my temper are equally renowned for how bad they are.

"You think you did that by yourself, Amanda?" He gestured to my pendant. "You had the power of a god behind you. *My* power. You couldn't have gotten anywhere on your own. My power propelled your writing. You said so yourself. My power compelled people to accept your work. My power made you."

"I was on my own here," I said, slamming my free hand into the cushioned seat for emphasis. "You were sucked through that portal, and I had no idea what had happened to you." I felt tears starting to well up on my lower lashes. My jaw clenched, and my throat tightened. I hated crying in front of anyone. It made me feel weak. But when I get so angry and have nowhere else to store my frustration, it spills out of my eyes.

"Oh, dear Morningstar," Ryley said with a sigh. He cupped my cheek with his palm and fingers, lightly brushing away my tears with his thumb. "I forget how difficult it must be to be a human. Don't be sad. I'm sure you're a fine writer."

He leaned in to kiss me, and I had to swallow hard to stuff that anger down as deep as I could get it in that moment. *Now is not the time, McDaniel.* By the time his lips met mine, I'd been able to get the cap on the emotional bottle, even as I could feel the pressure still building. I reminded myself of the Big Picture. Ryley would never concede a point, no matter how petty or important the matter was. And I needed Ryley for my plan to succeed. Without his cooperation, everything would go wrong in New Jersey, and I had no idea how bad that might be either for me or for the world. Instead, I let myself sink into the warmth and sensation of his kiss, allowing it to wash away any residual hurt feelings on my part.

"See?" he said, drawing back to refill our glasses. "We're going to have it all in a few short hours."

I nodded, not yet trusting myself to speak. Reflexively, I took another sip of the champagne but had lost all joy in the action.

"So, what is your big plan?" he said, lounging back against the seat. "You've never really come out with the details."

"That's because you never asked." As I spoke, I held his eyes over the rim of my glass, silently willing him to drop it. I finished my champagne about the same time Ryley polished off the remainder of the bottle. I was stalling for time because I did not need him interrogating my plan or rewriting it for more favorable terms. Unfortunately, my tactics only bought me a few minutes.

"I'm asking now," he said, making a show of finishing off the last his drink. "I've followed you this far. I'll need details if I am to play my part well."

I set my glass into the box, then took his glass and the bottle and did the same. Carefully, I walked him through the most basic details of my plan, if I could really call it that. It was more of a Hail Mary kinda mess.

"So, we get to the gate and transfer my power back to me. That's it." Ryley tilted his head a bit as he spoke. I could read the skepticism in his gesture.

"Yep. That's it. You get your power, and I am free of the madness in my life."

"And we're together."

"Exactly," I said with a firm nod, even though I didn't fully anticipate being alive at the end of the process. Gaining his cooperation wasn't really about trust. This was about success in the mission and to some extent survival, specifically, mine.

He watched me carefully. I'd left out the part about getting him through the gate once it was done. I had the power to call him to our world. I hoped I could be the morning star that lured him back to his eternal slumber with the same magic that called him forth from the ocean yesterday. Was it only yesterday? Having a malevolent god roaming the earth wasn't going to work for humanity. If I couldn't get back from the other side, well, I'd had a pretty good run. I couldn't risk Cthulhu in his full form rampaging across humanity.

But his incredulity showed me that he wasn't buying what I was selling. So I needed to push a harder sell.

I moved toward Ryley, crawling on top of him in the plush seat.

"Isn't that what you want, Ryley? You," I kissed his fore-head. "Me." I kissed the tip of his nose. "Together." I kissed him hard on the lips, eagerly deepening the embrace, and moved my hand down to cup his groin. It was like springing the latch on a puzzle box. I felt him harden beneath my touch, as I pulled back to tug at his lower lip with my teeth.

He rumbled in a feral growl and began hurriedly undressing me. Although I would have liked to have been smug about using his physical form to override his intellect, I was too far lost myself to care.

Now straddled across his lap, I pulled back so I could divest myself of my shirt and bra. As I did, Ryley unbuttoned and removed his own shirt. His hand slid into my hair. He grabbed hard slowly pulling my head back to give himself access to my neck. Slowly, Ryley nibbled and licked his way down my neck and collar bone, carefully crossing the meridian of my silver chain. He stopped to lavish attention on both breasts, suckling gently at each nipple, hardening them to the point of pain, before moving yet lower.

I felt his hands running down my back, forcefully holding my body to his mouth. Ryley nuzzled my stomach as he took a moment to undo the button and zipper on my jeans. In one smooth move, he removed them along with my panties and reset-tled between my legs. His human form made it possible for him to experience the sexual chemistry generated by skin to skin contact, and he never hesitated to take the opportunity to get me fully naked.

I wanted to say something. Something romantic. Maybe something profound. This was almost certainly our last time together, but Ryley's ministrations made speech impossible. Hands firmly on my backside, he hauled me up to his face, burying himself in me, tasting me, teasing me, devouring me. I could feel his fingers inside me, stroking the spot where he knew I couldn't control my reactions.

I clutched the crushed velvet of the seat, digging in deep enough to feel the springs. I could feel the tide of my emotions rolling over me, threatening to drag me under. In that moment, I could understand the worship, the utter devotion to him people must feel when they succumb to Ryley's influence. When the water is deep enough, you lose your orientation and can't find the surface. I was going under, tumbling as I fell. There wasn't enough air. I gripped his hair with both hands and screamed as orgasm after orgasm rolled through me in waves.

Looking down my sweat-slicked body, I saw Ryley lift his head and smile, a feral and altogether possessive gesture. He reared up onto his knees, his neck at a slight angle as his head was pushed into the roof of the car. He unbuttoned his jeans and pulled them down, not even bothering to remove them. Poised over me, he braced himself against the back of the seat and leaned down to insert his fingers again. Stroking me slowly at first, he built up the speed and pressure again. I could feel myself contracting again, coiling tighter and tighter. The build-up was becoming almost painful and as I struggled, Ryley looked down on me. I would have thought him unaffected except that his hair was damp from sweat and he was rock hard.

Not so unaffected after all.

"Ryley, please…"

I didn't need to say anymore. Ryley withdrew his fingers and moved on top of me, resuming the stroking as he entered me fully. Braced against the door of the car with his feet, he thrust harder and harder. I matched his rhythm as best as I could in the confined space. This time, when I came, screaming his name, he came too. Together we rode the tsunami to the fullness of its heights, and lay panting on the seat, enjoying the receding waves.

I couldn't say how long we laid there, just listening to each other breathe. Every now and then, I'd jump a bit, still feeling Ryley inside me, my body recalling our passion with tiny ripples. He called them "aftershocks," and he chuckled after every one until, at last, one of them expelled him from me.

When we were both sufficiently recovered, we began to gather our clothes and get dressed. It was a challenge in the relative confines of the backseat, despite it being a limousine. Since Ryley had been my first lover, I'd never had the teenage backseat experience so many of my peers had talked about. Now I saw both the appeal and the drawbacks. I felt like I was living my life on a delay sometimes, but if I was going to go out tonight, I was going to go out fully spent and with a smile on my face.

Ryley and I spent the rest of the ride mostly quiet. I tucked my feet up on the seat and leaned into him as we rode, enjoying the sights. Thanks to Friday rush hour traffic, it took us nearly two hours to reach our destination. The sun would set within the hour. By then, I was as calm as I could be under the circumstances. If Ryley felt any trepidation or questioned my intentions, he certainly didn't show it.

As the limo pulled up to Novastella Manor, I finished gathering my things and straightening my clothes as best as I could in the limiting confines of the limo's passenger area. Seeing the ivory-handled corkscrew still on the floor, I snapped it closed and placed it in my purse. I didn't know if I would need it later or not, but I didn't want to take any chances. I was a big believer in being prepared. If I got out of this alive, celebratory bubbly would definitely be in order.

Ryley watched as I organized, occasionally smiling at me as he straightened his own clothes.

"We'll be able to do this anytime we desire, Morningstar. Soon." He smiled again, as he buttoned his shirt.

I admit that my mood darkened a little between his use of my nickname and our proximity to the gate that was going to end things for us one way or another.

"We're going to retain our forms once we, uh..." I paused involuntarily, then hoped Ryley wouldn't notice, "...go through?"

"You know, I'm not entirely sure. I doubt it. But once we return my full powers to me, with your assistance," he said, gesturing to my necklace, "we should be able to move freely back and forth between R'lyeh and the surface world. Whatever form you have will be pleasing to me."

I knew he meant that to be reassuring. His ego also meant that of course I would find any form of his pleasing as well. Both ideas made my stomach churn with anxiety. I thought of the flash of the real Ryley that I saw through that gate 15 years ago. The tentacles. The burning red eyes. The square black pupils incapable of registering humanity as more than a virus. The horror. I took a deep breath and stuffed all of my emotions as deep as I could while trying not to imagine taking that form myself. It wouldn't go well for me if Ryley suspected I was having any second thoughts. Instead, I smiled and lightly tugged at a tendril of his beautiful hair, one rogue curl in front of his shoulder.

"I'm sure we'll be fine."

We exited the limousine and stood before the old house, which looked much the worse for wear. I slung my purse onto my shoulder, holding it tight to my body. I'd need its contents for the upcoming rituals. Ryley took my hand and started forward, but I resisted and cleared my throat.

"Your promise?" I gestured to the limo driver, still staring straight ahead blankly, having brought us here more or less on autopilot.

"Oh, yes. That. I forgot."

Still holding me with his right hand, Ryley used his left hand to open the passenger side door across from the driver. The driver turned toward him. The man's face changed to one of worshipfulness and adoration.

"You may go. Return to New York City and forget you ever came here. Forget you ever saw us," Ryley intoned in his deep and commanding voice.

I suppressed the chill that ran through me. That voice alone held power – it weakened my knees but not my resolve.

"Yes, my lord."

He began pulling forward before Ryley even closed the door. It swung shut with the momentum of the vehicle but was left partially latched and slightly ajar. The driver never made an attempt to completely close the door as he turned around in the semicircular drive and went on his way. I could see the door moving back and forth, neither fully latching nor opening, as he pulled away.

"Happy?" Ryley asked as he turned back to me.

"Yes, thank you." I had to acknowledge every thoughtful action. Without that small reward, he would stop doing them. I needed his full cooperation for what was next to come.

As he pulled me toward the porch, I resisted. "Can't we go around the house? Not through it?" I wasn't wanting to go into that house of horrors again. I could feel the anxiety welling up as I remembered the feeling of being chased out of it all those years ago.

"The side yard doesn't connect to the beach," he said, showing some exasperation at my questions. "You can only access the beach from the stairs, and you can only access them through the backyard, and you can only access that through the kitchen, and you can only access that…"

"Through the house," I finished for him.

"Exactly."

"But how could…" I trailed off remembering the twists and turns in the house itself, how it felt so much bigger inside than it should have been. "So, the house itself is a portal of sorts? Like a gateway to the gateway? Even time is different on both sides of the house?"

"Yes," he sighed, obviously growing frustrated with my curiosity. "To all of those. Mostly. It has more to do with time than distance. It's like the same place and the same reality but at a different time. Any other questions?"

"Uh, no. I'm good," I said. I wasn't, but I would have to pretend to be to keep Ryley from getting too irritated with me. What I really wanted to do was quiz him on all of the quirks of this damn house, but there was no time. Unfortunately, I desperately needed him to keep his guard down and not begin to doubt me, as I was beginning to doubt myself.

I looked up over the house. Even as twilight grew closer, there was still plenty of light left in the clear sky. Even now, just above the horizon line of the roof, I could see the faint twinkling of Trekkie, each star helping to create the five-pointed symbol of protection. I hoped it was the cosmos trying to protect our frail planet and its inhabitants from our upcoming ritual. I hoped it augured a favorable outcome.

But while I was hopeful, I was also a realist. That stupid prophecy kept rattling around in my head, promising world destruction because I'd brought Ryley back through to our world again. I didn't want that. I'd prepared for two rituals this evening. One would bind an evil god to me for eternity, and I would have to leave this earthly realm to save it from his destruction. The other would destroy my pendant, but I wasn't sure if that one would work. My life might be spared, but where would the power from the nautilus shell go if the vessel were destroyed? How would it affect Ryley, and what if the power transferred to him but kept him on this side of the portal?

"We'll be fine," Ryley said. He leaned over, swept a piece of my hair behind my ear, gently pulled my gaze from the skies, and kissed me on the forehead. "I promise."

Suddenly, this was the Ryley I fell in love with all those years ago, before the horror that I now knew him to be had been revealed. I couldn't help but wonder, though, if this softer, more reassuring tone had less to do with tenderness and more to do with him realizing that he needed my cooperation as well.

Hand-in-hand, we walked up to the door. I felt like that young college girl from 15 years ago, thinking I was off to meet his parents, approaching the threshold of their home. But these weren't his parents, and I was no longer that naïve. That telltale flutter in my stomach was still there. Instead of a flutter over possible embarrassment – saying the wrong thing, laughing too loudly, breaking some piece of heirloom dinnerware with a careless slip – this was a flutter of impending doom. Suddenly, I wasn't sure I needed to be rid of the insanity in my life. Maybe the power in my pendant would remain dormant. I didn't feel so gung ho about saving the world, and I wasn't sure I ever wanted to let go of Ryley's hand. We stepped onto the rickety porch and stood before the front door.

"Ready?" he asked.

"Absolutely," I lied.

He reached for the key over the door, but it wasn't there this time. In frustration, he went to rattle the doorknob, but it turned easily in his hand. The front door swung open silently. Someone had obviously greased the hinges since our last visit.

We turned and looked at each other.

"Seems like they may be expecting us," he said, his voice barely above a whisper.

That was not optimal. I shrugged. Nothing to be done for it now.

Despite feeling like we were walking into a trap, we crept in and closed the door behind us as quietly as we could. Ryley reached out for my hand again, as our eyes took a moment to adjust to the lack of sunlight. We stood together, assessing our surroundings. The only sounds I could hear were Ryley's breathing and my own heart pounding a military tattoo in my ears. With a slight squeeze of my hand, Ryley signaled that we should move forward.

Although I doubted they would want to try to stop us in the freakish maze of hallways, my heart still jumped a little each time we passed a doorway. No, if they were here and planning on stopping us, my money was on them making their stand on the beach itself.

We moved through the house without a flashlight this time, but subdued lighting made it possible to see anyway. The soft glow of gaslight illuminated our path as we made our way back to the kitchen.

Something had been bothering me all these years, and being in the house brought it to the forefront of my mind again. This would probably be my only chance to ask.

"Ryley," I whispered. "When we were here before, you said your room wasn't upstairs. Where was it?"

He paused our movement and turned to look at me. "In the basement, in a cell, under the house."

I let out an involuntary gasp. "They kept you in a cage?"

"Yes."

I wanted to ask more questions, but the look on his face, as well as our lack of time to explore any issues not related to our purpose this evening, made that impossible.

"I'm sorry," was all I could manage.

He turned and moved us along.

My stomach clenched as we finally entered the kitchen. I remembered that I had thought it resembled what I guessed a meat processing room might look like, what with the huge tables and crusted floor drains. Again, my memories were inconsistent at best when it came to that night 15 years ago. I wanted to fill in the gaps, since this might be my last chance to do so. I let go of Ryley's hand and moved fully into the kitchen for the first time.

Connected to the butcher block tables, I could see leather cuffs with buckles where wrists, ankles, and a human neck would go. Standing this close, I could see the hooks hanging from the ceiling were iron and not kept clean. Rust, at least I hoped it was rust, coated them, giving them a shabby, neglected appearance. Unfortunately, nothing about the kitchen or the hooks indicated a lack of use. The gleaming white marble table I'd glimpsed briefly was not as uniform as I'd thought. It was etched with runes and sigils, some of which I recognized from my studies. The etched lines and grooves were filled in with dark brown material. I didn't even want to guess what it was, and I certainly didn't want to acknowledge what it probably was.

I made the mistake of inspecting the big stone fireplaces on the outer wall. While I wasn't brave enough to look in the pot hanging from the fireplace crane, I did look at the grate on the floor of the second hearth. There were burnt bones that appeared to be ribs. Then I saw what looked pretty clearly like a human forearm, complete with a radius, an ulna, and a few chunks of burnt flesh. There were some rough knife cuts on the bone, although I didn't have the expertise to know if they were done before or after the fire was applied to the arm. That, it turned out, was my breaking point. It was all too much. I stepped away from the hearth so fast, my head spun. I retched and had to physically place my hand over my mouth to keep from vomiting.

"Don't go soft on me now, Morningstar."

I wanted to say, "Don't be an asshole, Ryley," but, again, I couldn't upset him this close to the finish line. Instead, I took a few deep breaths to regain my equilibrium and keep my late lunch down. I nodded, moved away from the kitchen tables, and back to him.

"Sorry," I said weakly. I shouldn't have taken the time to look around, and I knew that, but years of curiosity got the best of me. I also knew I would never have another chance to satisfy it. My research into their activities only answered so many questions. I knew human sacrifice was well within the scope of their activities, but I was guessing it was a crowd favorite judging by the amount of use this space had seen. Cannibalism was also a likelihood. This knowledge made me even less inclined to want to meet them on the beach, but the only way through was forward.

I silently braced for the disturbing backyard again and its hideous statuary. No telling what they may have added in the interim. I took Ryley's hand, and we exited into the backyard.

To a dark, moonless night.

The sky didn't appear black only because I could seemingly see every star, with Trekkie prominent nearly overhead. It felt odd to be viewing the backyard by starlight, but the stars of Trekkie shone bright enough to see general outlines. Even more than that once my eyes adjusted. It was not unlike the lighting in a planetarium, only there were no comfy chairs and no narrator to make sense of the heavens.

There was just a cold light and an increasingly agitated almost-god pulling me along to my fate.

CHAPTER 12

Sixteen Years Ago

"A t last, I've found you, my Morning Star."

Amanda startled as a young man spoke and placed his hand on her arm.

"Excuse me?" she said, pulling away from him. She pulled up a clipboard, which she held before her in a defensive position. She looked around, comforted by the fact that there were dozens of people milling around the Scales of the Universe exhibit with her.

The man looked confused and backed up a step. He put his hands out as if in supplication. "The Morning Star. I'm heeding your call," he said in a deep voice that softly stroked her ears.

For a moment, all she could do was stare. She thought he was the most handsome man she'd ever seen. He had the most arresting eyes – an unnatural shade of aquamarine, like the Caribbean Sea. His dark, wavy hair looked tousled and wind-blown, despite there being no breeze in the air-conditioned space.

"I don't really understand," she began.

She missed that he looked around quickly as if searching for the correct response. He pointed to the pale yellowish orb wedged between its sized-to-scale terrestrial siblings, Mercury and Earth. "I was looking for this. Venus, the Morning Star."

"Oh," Amanda said and chuckled nervously. "I thought... never mind. Are you doing the Astronomy Club scavenger hunt? I just got to this part of the exhibit myself." She held out her clipboard and an attached sheet partially filled out with answers.

"Yes, I was, but I lost my paper." He turned his hands, palms up, in a non-threatening gesture. "Perhaps we could share?"

"Sure," Amanda said, a little flustered by this attentiveness from a handsome stranger. "The American Museum of Natural History, even just the Hayden Planetarium part, is so much bigger than I thought it would be, but I've pretty much done everything else in Welcome Week over the years, so I thought I'd give this outing a try."

He nodded as she spoke, as if in agreement. He stared at her so closely. She felt herself flush a little at the attention. To break the tension, she said, "If we're going to be partners, I guess we should introduce ourselves." She tentatively put out her right hand. "I'm Amanda McDaniel."

The young man looked at her hand curiously. Eventually, he placed his left hand beneath hers, lifting it slightly, but not shaking it. His touch was gentle and warm, and Amanda thought she felt a slight tingle of electricity when they connected. He said something harsh and guttural, possibly in a foreign language, but Amanda was so caught up in the sensations of their physical connection that she didn't quite catch it. He had a strange accent she wasn't sure she'd heard before.

"I'm sorry, Ryley, is it?" she asked, repeating back a close proximity of what she'd heard but not wanting to offend him.

"Yes. In English." He paused then continued. "Ryley. Ryley Pacifica. A pleasure to meet you, Amanda McDaniel."

He continued to hold her with his intense gaze, her uplifted hand still supported by his. She felt like everything around them had been brought to a silent standstill while representations of the universe hung all about them. Finally, he smiled wide, breaking the tension while setting Amanda's heart aflutter anew.

"Are you ready to travel the Solar System with me?" he asked.

"Lead the way," she replied, unaware of the magnitude of his question and her response.

As he turned, he tucked Amanda's hand onto his arm and proceeded deeper into the planetarium.

Amanda and Ryley made their way through the exhibit, talking about the Solar System and the universe and the idea of traveling in deep space. Amanda did most of the directing, wanting to make sure they answered all the questions on the scavenger hunt. The prize was a $20 gift certificate to the student bookstore, and she could always use an extra boost with the cost of textbooks. They talked about space as Amanda completed their answer sheet. When they reached the end of the exhibit space, Ryley looked around perplexed.

"Why have they omitted Yuggoth?" He looked around as if he was missing a key piece of the astronomy lesson in the space.

"You mean Pluto?" Amanda asked. "They've decided it's not a planet anymore. It's a dwarf planet now."

"That's ridiculous! Of course, it's a planet."

"Dr. Neil deGrasse Tyson says it isn't, and he runs the place." Amanda laughed. "At least Pluto is uninhabited, so there's no one to complain about the oversight."

"The denizens of Pluto, especially the Mi-Go, would disagree with your hypothesis, but I take your meaning."

Amanda looked askance at Ryley. What was he going on about?

Then he smiled at her again, and all of her thoughts fled her mind. Amanda never believed in love at first sight or the idea of being hit by a lightning bolt out of the blue when you meet the Right One. She hadn't connected with any of her peers in high school or ever been attracted to anyone she'd met in college. In fact, she'd never felt such a closeness with someone in her life, even people she'd known for years, as she did with this man. And she'd just met this guy a few minutes ago.

"You want to catch the show in the planetarium with me, Ryley? It's the last section of the scavenger hunt."

"I'd be honored."

Amanda felt a little thrill as she settled into her seat in the darkness next to Ryley. Sitting so close, she could feel the warmth of him next to her. She thought he must be wearing a seriously intoxicating cologne because he smelled faintly of a crisp breeze coming off the ocean, and all she could think about was what it would be like to roll around in the sand with him. As they enjoyed the show, tilted back in their chairs to best view the artificial night sky, Ryley would occasionally whisper to her with an observation about the stars that would make her snicker or gasp. He would often punctuate what he said with a casual caress of her arm or by lightly touching her shoulder as he leaned into her. It only intensified her desire to be closer to him. It was making her fidgety. She tried to be quiet, but Ryley was telling a bunch of funny little stories about the planets and stars like he had traveled among them. She thought he should turn them into short stories for science fiction magazines, and she told him as much after the show.

Unlike Amanda, he declined any aspirations of being an author. "I just tell them to entertain you, Morningstar."

After the show, Ryley excused himself for a few minutes, suggesting that they meet up again in the restaurant area on the lower level. While she waited, she found the president of the Astronomy Club and submitted her scavenger hunt sheet. When she met up with Ryley again, he offered to buy her a late lunch before their tour of the planetarium concluded. Amanda had never enjoyed a meal more, although she was a little taken aback at how much Ryley ordered and ate. She kidded that he mustn't have had a decent meal in long time and chalked it up to the whole "starving college student" trope.

They parted ways after their late lunch. Ryley never asked for Amanda's number or anything else and, nervous that she was reading the signs wrong, she didn't offer any information. As she rode the train back to her dorm room, she thought about how nice it was to spend her afternoon with the handsome stranger and how chicken she was to have not offered her phone number.

When the semester started the following Tuesday, Amanda's first class was the only one she was dreading. Even though she focused on writing and majored in the Humanities, she had to take two general education science courses to finish out her senior year and graduate in May. Because it always made the most sense to her, and because Astronomy wasn't an option, she chose Biology for her two-class sequence. The only section that fit her schedule in the Fall was at 8 am, so on Day 1, she dutifully packed up her bookbag and made her way to the Biology building. She found a seat near the back at one of the empty lab tables and waited for class to begin.

Amanda had her head down in her journal, jotting down ideas for a short story when she became aware that someone sat down next to her. Not wanting to interrupt her train of thought, she hunched deeper into her work, ignoring the interloper that would likely be her lab partner for the semester. An inauspicious beginning to their working together, but she was intent on her fiction at the moment. She could exchange pleasantries at the break.

As she wrote, she thought she caught a faint whiff of salt, crisp like the winds off the ocean. Then she heard that deep timbre again.

"Good day to you, Morningstar."

Shocked, she looked up and gazed again into the clearest aquamarine eyes.

"Ryley! What are you doing here?" She inadvertently dropped her pen onto the table.

He nodded and smiled.

"Same as you. Taking Intro to Biology." He picked up her pen and handed it to her.

"Did you put off your science gen ed until senior year, too?"

He paused, but again, she didn't catch it.

"Yes. Yes, I did."

The professor walked in and passed out the syllabus, essentially beginning the class with little fanfare. She explained that students were now lab partners with the person seated at their table. She spent a few minutes pairing up people who were seated alone and rearranging those who wanted new accommodations. Amanda took the opportunity to speak with her new lab partner.

"You're going to need the textbook," she said, pointedly looking at the empty table in front of Ryley. "If you're looking for the lab partner that completes all of the group work while you do nothing, I'm not your girl."

"As you say, I'm in need of some supplies. I will be certain to have them by our next meeting."

And he did. By the following class, Ryley had a backpack, notebooks, pens, and the textbooks. He was a conscientious lab partner for Amanda, for which she was grateful. She had lied on the first day. She was totally the type of person who would do all the work to ensure an A. She just hadn't wanted to tip her hand.

Within a week, they were dating. Amanda was elated, as she had never dated before beyond a few movies with friend groups and some awkward kisses with boys who wanted more than friendship. But she'd never really clicked with anyone and, thus, never really dated a person exclusively. She was heady with the thrill of her first romance.

By the time midterms came around, things were getting serious; at least, that was how Amanda felt. She was comfortable enough with Ryley that she agreed to go to his apartment to study for their Biology midterm. She was pragmatic enough to bring a change of clothes stuffed in her backpack. She felt like this might be the time that she and Ryley finally took the next step in their relationship.

When she arrived to study, Ryley had already ordered a spread of Chinese food, which had been delivered just before she got there. His small dining room table was covered with Styrofoam clamshells, tiny holes melted through the tops, sides, and bottoms where hot fried food poked out, and at least a dozen quart-sized oyster pail containers, each with a different dish within. As she stepped in the door, the apartment smelled like a restaurant.

Her stomach growled in response.

Without the dining table available, they adjourned to the couch and opened their notes and books on the coffee table. They ate, studied, and talked for hours, going over the semester's labs and lessons so far. She couldn't put her finger on it, but something about the way he studied always gave her the impression this was all too easy for him.

By the time they finished, it was nearing midnight. Amanda packed up her books and began to tuck them into her backpack. When Ryley handed her notebook to her, he saw the clothes sticking out around her books.

"Why the extra set of clothes, Amanda?"

She sat a moment, frozen with mortification, she and Ryley each still holding a side of the notebook. She felt her face flush bright red. Even the tips of her ears burned.

"Uh. I just... I mean, I thought that maybe... if you wanted," Amanda stammered. "Nevermind. I didn't really think that..."

He released the notebook and placed his hand gently on her arm.

"Stay."

With that one word and a single intense look, her life was forever changed.

Amanda had worried that her lack of experience would make their first time awkward, but Ryley said nothing about that. Slowly at first and picking up speed and intensity with repeated rounds, they made love throughout the night. Only the insistent blaring of Ryley's alarm going off around seven the next morning enabled them to make it to their midterm in time. Although Ryley appeared unfazed by the lack of sleep, Amanda was a little worse for wear. However, what she lost in bleariness she more than made up for in giddiness. Plus, she really had studied hard and thought she'd done well despite her state.

Instead of parting ways after the exam, Ryley and Amanda returned to his apartment for more fun in bed and a much-needed nap. When they awoke again, he took Amanda out for an evening in the wider city.

They strolled around Central Park and ate dinner at a little hole-in-the-wall Chinese restaurant. While they were there, seated at one of the larger family tables, even though it was only the two of them, Ryley pulled a piece of cloth from his pocket and slipped it across the now nearly-empty table to Amanda.

"What's this?" she asked, accepting the small package.

"It's yours. Open it."

She unfolded the rough dark green cloth, noticing that the edges seemed to be torn and frayed rather than cut straight, only to find a nautilus shell on a long silver chain.

"Oh, Ry, it's beautiful!" She turned the odd shell over and over in her hands, admiring the strange whorls and patterns. It was unlike anything she'd ever seen before.

"May I put it on for you?"

Amanda nodded excitedly and handed it to Ryley. She bowed her head toward him a little.

He took the chain into his hands and stood up to formally

present his gift. "Amanda Melissa McDaniel, do you accept this pendant of your own free will and volition?"

She looked up, confused for a moment.

"Sure, I mean, yes, of course, I do."

"And do you accept this knowing that by receiving this pendant, you will be tied to me for all eternity in an unbreakable cosmic bond, as the stars are bound to the endless void of deep space?"

She chuckled and played along nervously. "Yes, forever and ever with you. I accept." She smiled, wondering what Ryley was going on about. He didn't usually play around like this.

Then she ceased thinking almost entirely when he smiled beatifically upon her.

"My Morningstar." He placed the chain over her head and settled the pendant on the front of her shirt, taking a moment to caress her skin down the length of the chain, barely brushing her breast, despite the public setting. "Now we shall be together. Always."

He leaned down. She could feel the heat of his body and smell that salty tang combined with a warm musky scent that she associated exclusively with Ryley. Without a care for any other patrons in the restaurant, he kissed her deeply and passionately where she sat.

As they left the restaurant, Ryley took the time to exchange pleasantries with the owner, Mr. Wang, while paying the bill. When they felt they had enjoyed enough of walking the city, Ryley flagged down a taxi to return them to his apartment. As they had the night before, the new lovers spent the night tangled in each other's embrace.

By the end of the semester, Amanda spent nearly as many nights in Ryley's apartment each week as she did in her dorm room. Somehow, she managed to keep her head above water long enough to complete her studies and graduate the following May. Ryley graduated with her, and neither of them had family in attendance at the graduation. Instead, he told her that after graduation, they should travel the world before settling into any careers.

She thought that sounded as exotic and exciting as anything she'd ever heard before. She was already planning a Kerouacesque road journal of their adventures together. She was hoping to try to get it published when they got home. Ryley told her the last thing he needed to do before they could embark on their journey was to make a quick trip to his ancestral home in New Jersey to pick up his passport; then the world would be theirs to command.

CHAPTER 13

I looked forward to the time I would never have to see Novastella Manor and its many domestic aberrations again. Stumbling from the kitchen of horrors into the backyard, I looked up to the sky in confusion. While it was nearing sunset when we entered the house, now it was dark, well past sunset and even twilight.

"We were only in the house for a few minutes, Ry. It looks like midnight out here."

"I told you, the side yard doesn't connect to the beach or the backyard."

"That's right. Same place, different time," I said sheepishly.

"Can we get moving again, Morningstar?"

I nodded my acquiescence but remained in place while I got my bearings.

In the darkness, I could just make out the outline of the stone gate down on the beach, which I now knew to be a portal to Ryley's underwater city. But not at this moment, not until it was activated. I smelled the salinity of the air and heard the sound of the waves breaking on the sand. These sensations washed over me like a balm, bringing a moment of clarity and calm to an otherwise unhinged scenario. The odd lighting, reflecting off the beach below, as well as concerns over my possible impending death, must have turned my thoughts to the dramatic because it brought to mind a few lines from my favorite piece of literature.

"Ghastly grim and ancient Raven wandering from the Nightly shore — Tell me what thy lordly name is on the Night's Plutonian shore."

At first, I didn't even realize I'd actually said it out loud. Ryley looked at me. Even he apparently realized how odd it was to have me suddenly reciting poetry before we proceeded to the beach. He was probably worried I was cracking under the tremendous pressure.

Maybe I was.

"It's Edgar Allan Poe," I said, defending my flight of fancy. "'The Raven.' One of his best works, I think," I said, still holding his hand, still scanning the shoreline, though, for what, I couldn't have said in the moment.

"Is Poe a contemporary of yours?"

I laughed, caught off guard by such an odd question. "No," I said. "I read all of his works in college, including his literary criticism and his journalism articles. He was a pretty great writer." Then I thought a second about the tone of his question. "Is Poe a contemporary of *yours* somehow?"

"I met the man once in a dream," Ryley said in a casual tone. "I couldn't remember if it was before or after I dreamed of you."

It was his turn to laugh.

"I remember that dream because in it there was a shantak on the beach, and I wondered how it came to be there. I also remember it because Poe was an odd sort. He didn't actually seem concerned or frightened or even particularly put out as he wandered my beach. He carried a book with him, as I recall." Ryley's gaze was distant as if he too was back on that beach, remembering. "When he entered R'lyeh, he walked right up to my temple and introduced himself with a bow and a flourish. He asked where he was and how he could return home again. I pushed one word into his mind, thinking to break him. 'Nevermore,' I believe it was. Then he faded away. I suppose he did stumble across a way out after all."

For a moment, all I could do was gape at Ryley. After everything that I had seen, studied and survived, was this the thing that was going to push me over the edge? That Ryley had somehow met Edgar Allan Poe?

Releasing his hand, I sat down hard on a cement bench. I closed my eyes and tried to center myself. I needed to not think about this. I needed to concentrate on the ritual ahead.

For once, Ryley didn't provoke or prod me to get moving. He gave me my space, and I was grateful. When I felt as close to normal as I was going to get, I stood up and took his hand again. "Let's get this done."

We walked through the garden and past the statue of the octopus-headed man, which I now knew was a statue of Ryley in his true form. Apparently, in the intervening years, someone had taken a hammer to the statue, vandalizing it.

"Randall," Ryley growled out, clenching his teeth when he saw the damage.

It was his turn to break from me to explore. He circled the statue, assessing the damage. Several tentacles had been chiseled off. Although there were some large chips missing from the body, it was the face of the statue that took the worst of the hammer blows. The nose was missing, and the eyes had been gouged out, leaving cracks in the face of it. Ryley leaned in close to inspect the statue without touching it. Finally, he rocked back a bit, as if taking it all in, judging the statue and its state in their entirety.

"He will pay for his insolence and disrespect, even as he pays for hurting you." Turning from the defaced work, Ryley returned to my side. "I look forward to confronting him on that accursed beach once I have my powers back in full."

We resumed picking our way down the path toward the staircase to the beach. Little else in the backyard had changed beyond the damage to Ryley's statue. Perhaps it was a little more overgrown and shaggy, but I couldn't recall enough about its appearance in the past to be sure. The first time I'd come through here, I was with Ryley, and everything was new. I was love-blind to the strangeness of the entire place. The second time, though, I'd been running for my life, literally not seeing the garden or its stone inhabitants in my desperation to get away. Even now, with the faint light and my mind on the rituals ahead, I wasn't as observant of my surroundings as I should have been. I couldn't concentrate or bring myself to care because I was convinced our trouble would be on the beach.

We approached the stairs, and my stomach clenched. They were still the same rickety, rattle-trap affair I remembered, although I couldn't see all the way down due to a lack of lighting. Looking past them, I couldn't make out any figures on the beach, which only made me more nervous.

Ryley, possibly sensing my hesitation, stepped onto the stairs first, gently pulling my hand.

"Think of something besides the descent," he said. "That will help you."

"Like what?" I asked, cautiously placing my weight on the little landing at the top and feeling it rock under my feet, shifting slightly. I gripped Ryley's hand harder, as my other hand shot out to clutch the equally wobbly railing.

"Oh, I don't know." He tugged a little more forcefully and began leading me down the stairs. "Perhaps you'd like to know more about my city, our new home. Of course, we won't be trapped there. You'll keep me awake, and we can travel. Would you like to hear a story about traveling among the stars? You used to enjoy those."

I only half-heard what he was saying. I just started moving, going down two whole steps, when a thought popped into my head.

"Yeah, okay, actually, I have a question. What the hell is a shantak?"

He paused on the stair ahead of me, which also brought me to a halt, and cocked his head to the side as if he wasn't entirely sure what to make of my line of questioning.

"Well, it's…" He paused.

I could read his face. He was prescreening his answer to decide what would best satisfy me without upsetting me, as he tried to coax me forward with light pulls. I didn't budge.

"I suppose a big blackbird is the closest description I could give you. Or a bat. But a huge one. Like you could ride them if you could catch one. Maybe a dragon would be closer. I'll try to find one to show you. They don't typically find their way to R'lyeh."

All I could do was stare at him. Big black bird bat dragons. Excellent. This whole night was becoming even more surreal than I had expected, and that was saying something. If I survived the ritual, this would be what my life would be like all the time. I wasn't sure if I could handle it or if that would even matter.

"Thank you," I finally managed.

Instead of saying anything more, he again pulled at my hand to indicate we should keep moving. The stairs swayed slightly with each step we took, and my stomach felt like it was mimicking the motion.

We worked our way down the rest of the stairs in silence. I was not in the mood to be distracted, and he apparently was no longer in the mood to ease my concerns. I could feel the tone of our journey shifting from a lover's adventure to the deadly serious business it truly was.

We made it down to the beach without incident and, although we weren't trying to be stealthy, there was no one waiting for us at the bottom. Between that and getting off those damn stairs, my relief was nearly overwhelming. Now it was time to cross the beach – our last trial before the ritual.

Although it was fewer than 100 yards from the stairs to the stone arch, it felt like an eternity. As we moved across the sand, we were totally exposed. Without voicing our strategy, both of us swiveled our heads, on the lookout for enemies. I really felt this was where Randall and his merry band of lunatics would make their attack. The bright starlight radiated down onto the beach, illuminating the arch. The odd gold flecks in the dark arch caught the faint light and twinkled like tiny stars in the stone.

I might have thought it beautiful if I didn't know that the arch opened a portal to a horrible world, and its very stones had been steeped in blood to make that happen. My research was clear on that point. Blood, copious amounts of it, activated the portal. It was the reason there was a small dagger in my bag. One or both of us were going to have to give until it hurt, literally.

When we finally reached the arch, there still wasn't a cultist in sight.

"Set up and do your magic," Ryley said in a gruff tone. "I'll keep a lookout for Randall."

Although I was in no mood to listen to orders barked at me, I couldn't afford to make anything of it. Time was of the essence, which I knew even better than Ryley.

"On it," was all I said.

I pulled out my bag of protection and set it at my feet. It would be my companion as I worked. Next out was the dagger, which I used to etch runes and sigils into the wet sand. I was just putting out some other components when Ryley spoke up.

"Put up a protection spell or something. And hurry. We haven't got all night," he snapped.

At this, I drew another, more figurative line in the sand.

"I can't put up a protection spell because you blow through it with your presence. I discovered that when I called you yesterday, so that's a waste of time," I explained. "And I am going as fast as I possibly can. Your backseat magicking isn't helping."

"My what?"

"Never mind."

I continued to place my components in and around the sigils. Reading the situation, I decided to prep the transference spell instead of the one to destroy my pendant. Of all the things Ryley knew, the spells and rituals were probably a mystery to him, as they were usually performed in his absence. At least, I hoped this was true, as it gave me the smallest advantage over him. I was concerned that if he realized I was doing something destructive, he would retaliate or at least stop me for an explanation, for which we didn't have time. I also didn't think I would have time to do the backup spell correctly, and I couldn't be sure what would actually happen if the nautilus, still containing Ryley's power, were to be destroyed. I couldn't chance a catastrophe. I already had to get a portal spell right, and I was worried that I didn't have the power or capability to pull off three spells in a row. Transference it would have to be; then I would have to lure Ryley through the portal and out of our world. His power would be returned to him, but he would be unable to get back to our world to wreak havoc and cause the prophesied chaos.

It was unlikely I could make it back. I was going to take one for Team Humanity.

I allowed myself a sigh of remorse, then pushed the negative thoughts away to concentrate on my task at hand. Finally, when I had everything set up according to my research, it was time. I made another scan of the low-lit beach, even though Ryley had been on watch duty. I set down the dagger I'd used to score the sand.

"Okay, Ryley. Let's do this."

I moved him into his place for the ritual, positioning him standing in the now inert archway, with his hands pressed into either side. I took the opportunity to enjoy one last instant with him. Running my hands across the expanse of his chest, then twining my arms around his neck, I kissed him.

I kissed him hard.

I kissed him with every ounce of love college-age me possessed for him before I learned his secrets.

I kissed him with every bit of passion I felt for him now before he learned my secrets.

He returned my ardor, and we enjoyed one tender but fierce moment where we could just be our imaginary selves: two star-crossed lovers embarking on a desperate attempt to break free together. Only he thought this was the beginning of our grand adventures, and I knew it was the end.

"For luck," I whispered, as I disentangled from Ryley.

"We won't need luck, my Morningstar," he said, tenderly caressing my lower lip with his thumb before returning his hands to the archway. He smiled down and shifted his stance to physically occupy the most space in the portal. "We'll have each other. Forever."

I nodded my silent acquiescence, not trusting myself to speak in that moment.

I reached into my purse for the last spell component I needed. I'd crafted it specifically for this spell. It was an iron key with sprigs of rosemary braided around it. The writings about the ritual only specified an iron key, but I added the rosemary for luck in travel. I figured I would take any advantage, real or illusory, that I could get. I also picked up the dagger I'd left on the sand.

Taking my place before Ryley, I faced him and the portal.

"Okay, Ry, all you have to do is stand there. I'll do the rest. Keep an eye out for Randall and his crew, and alert me if they're inbound. If it's the start of the spell, I might be able to divert some energy to deflect them. Once I'm in the heart of the ritual, though, I can't do much to defend myself or you. Understand?"

"Once I have my power back, there will be no need to defend

me," Ryley said, bristling a little at my reminder of his current human vulnerability.

"Right, okay." I took one last moment to look into his eyes, his beautiful Caribbean blue human eyes. Impulsively, I kissed him lightly, no more than a peck on the lips, but I flicked my tongue out to taste him just a little, one final time. I was pretty sure I would no longer be interested or even capable of enjoying him on the other side of the portal.

I took a deep breath and began.

Holding the key before me in my left hand, with the dagger in my right, I commenced my chanting. Strange sounds emitted from my throat while my tongue worked to produce the horrible and awkward syllables I'd painstakingly memorized. Undertaking the casting of magic was hard enough, but doing it in an alien language was nearly impossible. I was all too aware that a simple slip or a transposition of words could invite my immediate doom.

As I spoke, the various sigils I'd dug into the sand flared up and glowed an incandescent green. When I completed the first part, the rosemary-laced key dissolved in my hand, blowing past Ryley to the opening of the archway. When that dust broke the plane of the opening, the entire archway lit up with the same green glow as the sigils, and beyond Ryley, I could see that other, hostile world, shimmering like a heat mirage. I could see across the ocean to a dark city on a moonlit shore. On the other side, the moon must have been full because it was almost as bright as daylight, except the light shone cold and harsh, as opposed to the warmth of the sun. There was only the slightest barrier between our two worlds, and I needed to breach it.

My fate laid bare before me, my stomach dropped.

"Team Humanity," I whispered to myself. I cut my left hand with the dagger, then cut the back of Ryley's hand in quick succession. I placed my palm over his wound and pressed, eliciting a slight grunt of pain from him, releasing our blood together, which was eagerly soaked up by the stone.

The barrier fell, and I caught a whiff of the squalid smell of the ocean and rot emanating from the other world carried on a light breeze. Unlike the opening of the portal years ago, there were no violent winds or crashing water, no vacuum effect, and no blast to announce the rift between the worlds. There was simply a veil dropping away and a clear view of the other side. This opening was perhaps all the more terrifying for its disingenuous mundanity. There was simply no longer a boundary between here and there.

Shaking off the feeling of foreboding, I began the second and more dangerous ritual.

My plan was to start the transference of power from my pendant to Ryley, then push him through the portal using my own body as the momentum. He would regain his power on the other side, but the act of both of us going through would seal up the portal, thereby saving the world. It wasn't a great plan, but it was the only one I could manage that ended with him on that side and humanity safe from his powers.

This time, when I began chanting, it was my pendant that began to glow. I picked carefully through the unwieldy sounds and accompanying motions, gesturing with the dagger. As I reached the critical juncture where the power would begin to transfer to Ryley, he spoke up.

"Randall and his minions just broke from the edge of the beach. They're coming this way. Hurry up!"

I shook my head as I sustained my chant, afraid of breaking the spell if I spoke to him.

"You have to go faster, Morningstar! He's closing!"

Trying to ignore Ryley, I continued my quest. A few more words and gestures, and this would be over.

"They're forming a semi-circle around us. Faster!"

As I persisted unabated, I could feel a new energy in our

vicinity. Whatever the cultists were doing felt like fire at my back, like they'd turned up the temperature on the entire beach. It felt like even the sand was radiating heat. Although I was sweating, I kept going. A cold, malodorous breeze wafted through the portal and over us, a thermal counterpoint to the malevolence behind me.

Facing forward, I saw Ryley's eyes changing. Gone was the tranquil aquamarine, and in its place, a hideous red, with squared, jet black pupils. The god was coming to the fore.

"Randall, I command you to stop!" Ryley bellowed in a voice so deep it vibrated in my chest, although I didn't know why until it was too late.

Even though I had only felt this particular type of pain once in my life, I recognized it immediately. Randall had stabbed me.

Again.

At first it felt like a punch, then I suffered the familiar searing pain as his dagger sliced through my organs. He hit me so hard I fell forward into Ryley. I managed to hold the dagger flat, so I didn't stab him, but he bellowed as the pendant made contact with him, pressed between us. I felt the weight of Randall pushing me forward, and I saw his left hand brace on the archway. It was like he was inserting himself into our ritual and completing the circuit as the energy coursed from the pendant and into our unholy threesome.

When he made that connection, however, all of my pain blissfully stopped. It was like there was no knife in me at all.

My relief was momentary, as I felt the wholly unwelcomed sensation of Randall's erection pressed against my backside through my jeans. He'd laid his head on my shoulder and was breathing heavily, obviously aroused by his contact with the archway and with us.

I turned to look at him. I could smell his hot, foul breath and saw a few locks of his greasy dark hair matted to his forehead.

He was moaning and thrusting himself into me as he rode the connection.

"Ia ia, Morningstar! Come with me! Be the concubine I deserve!" he cried out, grinding his wretched hard-on against me. Then his eyes flew open as if in total surprise.

"Your eyes!" he cried out. "They're red. You are a goddess!"

Instead of being repulsed, he apparently found this change a turn on, as his thrusts went to double-time.

The next few things happened in rapid succession.

Absent any pain, I managed to push off from Ryley with my right hand, keeping my left on the arch over his and Randall's hand on top of mine. I finished the spell, and green light flowed through the three of us, illuminating the sand beneath us and, I assumed, the rest of the beach as well. The ritual was complete, and the power was fully in play.

I managed to turn my body sideways to Ryley and, infused with the power of a god, punched Randall full-on in his face over my shoulder, using the dagger handle like a roll of quarters. Although I'm sure my energized punch would have killed a normal man, Randall was riding the same high as I was. His eyes were red, too. He did stagger back, dropping to one knee. I felt Randall's dagger tug downward then pull out as he recoiled from my hit. My blood flowed out onto the sand and ran like a river to the arch, only to disappear into its surface. A curious green ichor leaked out with my blood, greedily soaked up by the arch as well.

Although Randall's hand broke from ours, he managed to keep contact with the arch and maintained his green aura. He was still a part of the connection.

Ryley glanced down at Randall then back to me, staring intently into my eyes.

"I will fulfill my promise to you, my Morningstar."

Placing his left hand on my shoulder for connection, Ryley released his grip on the arch, reached out, and grabbed Randall by his throat. He lifted the dazed cult leader off the sand so they were face to face, Randall choking and gasping to breathe, his red eyes bulging out at the abuse.

"Let's see how you enjoy the hospitality in my home, as I once did in yours," Ryley said, low and menacing. Without another word, he flung Randall behind him and through the portal. Randall screamed, and it could still be heard even as he was hurled into the other world.

That action, however, came at a cost. Ryley found he could not pull his arm from beyond the plane of the portal, although we were still connected and sharing his power. He struggled to pull free, but it was obvious that what made it through the portal stayed anchored on the other side.

"Morningstar! Let us return to R'lyeh where my powers can manifest in full, and we can heal you."

I dropped my hand to my side in a futile effort to staunch the bleeding. Although I felt no pain, once again, I could feel my life running out of the gash Randall's dagger made in me.

"I don't know...I don't think I can..." It was getting harder to breathe.

'I need you, Morningstar. Without you, I won't be able to stay awake. I will not slumber again!" Ryley pulled at me with his one free hand, physically imploring me to come through the portal with him.

If I went through, I might survive, but for what fate, I couldn't even guess.

If I stayed, my chances weren't good. I would probably die on this beach right here next to this wretched portal.

It really didn't take much effort to decide.

One hand bloodied and one still clutching my dagger, I reached down to the silver chain around my neck and removed my pendant. As I pulled up the necklace, I could see my left hand was covered with both blood and toxic green-colored goo. I looped the chain over Ryley's head and let the pendant rest against his chest, the little nautilus powerless and pale grey.

"Nevermore," I said, shoving him with both hands to his chest. I pushed with everything I had left in me and enjoyed the brief satisfaction of seeing Ryley's shocked expression as he fell backward into the portal. I dropped to my knees and frantically gouged the sigils with my dagger, breaking the spell and closing the portal.

I was surprised to see the towering stones still held a faint glow. I looked at the sand, seeing that the thin red line still running from my body remained drawn to the sanguinary stones. There was no longer anything green coming from my body. I was on my own. The pain was back, too, much to my dismay. Feeling weaker with each passing moment, I groped for my purse, still on the sand near me. I picked up my bag of protection and clutched it tightly with one hand as I dug through my purse for a few components with the other. I was hoping there was enough to do another transference spell. I reached to my chest for the familiar comfort of my pendant, only to remember it was no longer there.

With no other hope left, I began to chant anew. I felt slow and sluggish as I formed my mouth and tongue around the strange syllables once again. I made the gestures with my hands, but it felt like I was doing everything underwater, with resistance to every movement. When I reached the end of the spell, I leaned forward, bracing both of my hands against the stone.

"I've given you everything, damn it," I cried out as I touched the arch. "Transfer back to me what is rightfully mine!"

I felt a tingle and watched, amazed, as the green glow drained from the stone and into my hands. When I saw no trace of green left in the stone, I pulled back and cradled my hands together, cupping the light like liquid. Carefully, I transferred as much of the glow to my wounded side as I could, trying to rub it into the damage like a salve. When I pulled my hands up to check, the glow was gone, replaced by my own smeared blood. I noticed the stones of my new ring coated with gore.

I could only hope it had helped.

Above me, Trekkie flared brightly, then winked out of existence. Astronomers all over the planet must have lost their collective shit in that moment. If I wasn't so busy bleeding and nearly dying, I might have been equally astounded. As it was, it only just registered in my consciousness.

I managed to stagger to my feet, hoping to find some assistance for my wounds. Instead, I turned to see the cultists, still in their semi-circle, staring at me with naked hatred.

Obviously, I hadn't thought this through.

I backed closer to the gate, buying me a moment to think, but one of the cultists charged me. As his feet were chewing up the distance in the sand, I figured that these people were so accustomed to following orders that it just might slow their assault if I tried commanding. I threw my hands out in front of me and yelled, "Stop!"

Although the cultist's feet kept propelling him forward, his head disappeared in a red mist. The corpse dropped at my feet, spraying me with blood.

After everything else I'd gone through, this was the step over the line. This was the moment my psyche decided I'd had enough. I dropped to my knees and threw up on the beach.

At that, the scene became even more chaotic. The cultists turned and scrambled to get away from me. I was looking at my hands, trying to figure out how I did that when I saw figures rappelling down the beach cliff from the backyard. I could hear popping sounds as more of the cultists hit the ground around me, blood pooling around them before soaking into the sand.

So it wasn't me.

Taking cover next to the gate, I watched as the figures from the cliff took shape. They wore black helmets with visors, black uniforms with black armored vests covering their chests, and they were carrying what appeared to be assault weapons. They looked like a military force. As they moved closer, I could see "ATF Police" emblazoned across their chests in big, white letters. The cavalry had arrived.

Randall's men scattered like the cockroaches they were.

Moving across the beach with military precision, the ATF agents cut off the cultists' retreat, shooting anyone that didn't drop to the ground at their advance and their shouted orders to lay down any weapons. The mayhem was over in minutes. The few surviving cultists were rounded up, forced to lay on their stomachs, and handcuffed.

One of the agents slowly approached me; his weapon pointed at the sand. "Ms. McDaniel, are you injured?" he asked.

"Well, yeah, my side," I began, but when I felt the area to show him, I realized that there was no longer an open wound where there had been one just a few minutes ago. I stood up and stepped away from the arch. "Actually, no, I'm good, thanks."

He looked at me quizzically, apparently confused by my answer. There I stood before him, my shirt sliced and slashed to hell; my jeans soaked with my own blood, stiffening and molding to my body as they dried; and my shoes painted red with my damage like a crime scene, but no, I was fine.

The hell of it was that it was true. I really was fine. There was no longer a gash in my side, and the pain was completely gone. Whatever that green glow had been, the last of Ryley's mojo or some residual godlike power, it had apparently done the trick. The worst of the damage was gone.

"The asset is secure, Sir," he said into his headset. He made a skeptical face at me before addressing his superior again. "No, Sir, she seems unharmed."

By this time, several other agents were milling around the area.

"Asset?" I asked. I kept one eye on him as I scooped up my bag of protection and placed it into my purse, which was still just sitting on the sand. I reached for the dagger, but the agent bent down and took it before I could.

"Sorry, evidence, ma'am," he said, handing the dagger to another agent walking by us.

"Sure," I said. "Won't be needing that again." I hoisted my purse onto my shoulder, feeling some comfort from its familiar weight. "What's next?"

"Please come with me," was his only response as he took me by the elbow and led me away from where the cultists were being held and back to the base of the stairs to the backyard. "Please wait here. Someone will be with you shortly."

Feeling exhausted from my recent exploits, I sat down heavily on one of the bottom steps. Rummaging through my purse, I discovered a mini plastic water bottle I'd caged from the hotel. The first few sips I swirled in my mouth and spat into the sand. The next few sips tasted better than the champagne I'd had earlier. I reached down to fuss with my pendant for comfort, again forgetting that it was no longer there. Not really ready to think about what had just happened, I sipped my water and watched small waves roll onto the beach. It was still pretty dark, so I was also distracted by the strobe-like effect of the ATF agents scanning the beach with flashlights as they rounded up the cultists. It was a little disorienting, and I'd already had quite enough of that for the night. I closed my eyes and listened to the sounds of the ATF's activities.

When I opened my eyes again, I found that to hasten their search, they set up portable lighting, illuminating the beach properly. It wasn't really an improvement from my vantage point. Now I could see the dark spots in the sand where cultists had died. I could see trenches dug in the sand by the feet of cultists being removed from the beach, dead and alive, dragged or still kicking. One of the lights was pointed directly at the arch, and several of the agents seemed to be inspecting it. They freely wandered through it and around the pillars since it was no longer opened to another world. They were careful to step around the gouges I'd made in the sand to destroy the sigils and magic powering the gate, probably trying to preserve evidence.

I couldn't imagine how they would explain this in their official reports.

After a few minutes, I spotted an older man in an ATF uniform down the beach. He wasn't wearing a helmet or an armored vest, and his short-cropped greying hair stood out among the younger-looking agents. He walked toward me like a tourist enjoying a stroll on the beach, casual, seemingly without a care. His demeanor didn't change a whit as he approached me.

"Ms. McDaniel, I'm Commander Beaudreau, ATF Special Response Team. The Federal Government and the ATF are glad to see that you were not greatly harmed during your ordeal," he said in a soft Southern drawl wholly out of place on this godforsaken Jersey beach.

"My agent informed me you were unhurt." He gestured to my side as he spoke. "Is that your blood?"

"No. It was... It was from one of them," I lied, not wanting to get into the specifics of things I couldn't possibly explain, and he couldn't possibly understand.

"I'm just glad we got here in time to stop them."

"M-m-me, too," I agreed. Whether it was from the chill of the night or the adrenaline wearing off, I began to shiver, my teeth rattling.

"This should help, Ms. McDaniel," Beaudreau said, removing his jacket and placing it around my shoulders.

"Thank you." My relief was immediate as I curled into the jacket, which smelled vaguely woody and of warm spices. It was pleasant, comforting, and a welcomed dash of normalcy, but I still had some questions for Beaudreau. "How did you know I was here, Commander? And why are you and your agency here?"

"I would expect an author and researcher such as yourself to have plenty of questions, and I hope I can answer them all to your satisfaction, ma'am," he said, chuckling a little. "We have had eyes on this terrorist organization for months now. We had intel that they were going to do something big tonight, but we didn't have specifics. We're just glad we got here in time, you weren't hurt, and they couldn't complete their plans. Another Waco situation would not look good for us."

All I could do was nod at his answers. I was definitely getting tired, and I just wanted this whole thing to be over. Apparently, Beaudreau sensed it as well.

"Now, if you will, Ms. McDaniel, please come with my agents and me. We are going to need to debrief you. I hope you understand?"

"Of course," I agreed. I gathered up my purse, slinging it over my shoulder.

He called over an agent to help me and, together, we managed to climb up the staircase. From the top of the bluff, I could see all sorts of ATF activity – cultists being rounded up by agents, agents collecting evidence from the beach, Beaudreau making his way up the steps some ways behind us. Although I could have used a break, there was no way I was stopping to rest until I was out of this lunatic hellhole.

We walked through the backyard as I diligently ignored the statuary, even the defaced image of Ryley as a god. The young agent escorted me through the house. I averted my eyes as we crossed through the kitchen. Even keeping my eyes down, I saw blood smears on the floors as if the ATF's clean-up had taken place throughout the house. As we stepped onto the porch, I could see that night had completely fallen on this side of the house as well, but it was also lit up by the ATF's temporary lighting rigs.

In the semi-circular driveway were at least a dozen black SUVs, unmarked but identical with tinted windows. Some were parked on the lawn, and all of them were facing out for a fast exit.

"Where exactly are we going, agent?" I asked, a creeping feeling of dread making the back of my neck tingle.

"Headquarters, ma'am," he answered curtly.

"Are we driving all the way to DC tonight?"

This time he didn't answer me. Instead, he kept leading me toward the second SUV, taking me to the passenger side. I saw that all of the SUVs had Louisiana license plates instead of federal plates. Uneasy, I glanced back toward the house one last time as the agent opened the rear car door for me to enter.

Commander Beaudreau was just stepping onto the porch as a small contingent of ATF agents holding one of the cultists approached from the side yard. The green-robed cultist, previously docile, went berserk when he saw the Commander, kicking and wriggling to get free of his captors.

"Dominique Laffite, you murdering bastard! I should have known this was your work. You ruined everything! Randall should have killed you when he had the chance."

Anything else the man had to say was cut short as the Commander stepped off the porch, unholstered his sidearm, and fired. The bullet caught the cultist directly between the eyes, ending his struggle.

My brain finally caught up. I realized these guys weren't the Feds, they weren't here to save me, and I wasn't going for a debriefing.

"You dumb sons-a-bitches. I told you to eliminate them all, not take prisoners." The Commander's fury caused his Louisiana patois to thicken, peeling back the veneer of civility he'd shown.

"Sir, I thought…"

"Your mission is not to think but to follow my every word," he said to the agent, his voice cold and calm. With that, the Commander fired again, twice. The impact snapping the agents' heads back, dropping them both as well as the body they held between them.

While the agent's attention was drawn to the commotion, I reached into my purse, momentarily forgetting my dagger was gone. Instead, I found the ivory-handled wine knife we'd gotten in the limo on the way here. Hand still in my purse, I opened the corkscrew, grasping the handle, so the spiral stuck out between my middle and index fingers.

Everything that happened next felt like a blur, like a horrible dream where you are being chased, but your legs are so heavy you can hardly move forward.

I took a deep breath and pulled the implement from my purse. Quickly, so I didn't have to think it through, I rammed the corkscrew into the agent's eye, twisted, and pulled. I dropped the bloody, meaty mess and pushed the door forward, knocking him to the ground.

His screams echoed in my ears as I let go and opened the door of the SUV next to us. I threw my purse onto the passenger seat and jumped into the driver's seat. I pulled the door closed and hit the locks. Hoping luck was on my side just this once, I pulled down the visor.

And a set of keys fell into my lap.

I could see the agents, or the cultists, or whoever the fuck they really were, running toward the SUV. Beaudreau, or Laffite, just stood still, watching me. We made direct eye contact, and I thought I caught him smiling.

I returned my attention to the task at hand and started up the SUV. The engine roared as I slammed the transmission into Drive and stomped on the gas pedal. I felt a jolt as I drove over the man I'd maimed, but I didn't let up on the accelerator even a little. Tearing down the driveway felt very déjà vu. I was covered in blood, driving a stolen vehicle while being chased by a madman.

I slammed on the brakes to make the turn out onto the road.

Sparing a brief glance at the rearview mirror, this time the woods weren't closing in behind me, but I could see the Commander, in the distance, watching.

I fishtailed out onto the road and punched it again. I had to swerve to get around some heavy equipment, a bulldozer and a construction crane on flatbeds coming towards me, taking up more than their lane. But in the end, seeing no one on my tail, I made it onto the Garden State Parkway and headed north to get the hell out of New Jersey.

W hen Amanda stole the SUV and started down the driveway, a dozen assault rifles came up and took aim on her.

"Hold your fire!" The commanding voice rang out through the yard, and every man complied immediately, pointing their weapons at the ground.

"Sir, why?" one of them risked asking, despite just seeing two of his comrades cut down for not following orders.

"She's still my daughter, and no harm will come to her," Dominique said.

"Sir, yes, sir."

"I'm sorry you had to see that, cher," Dominique smiled a little at the rapidly escaping vehicle. "You do drive like a hellion. Resourceful too. You do your Daddy proud, girl."

They all watched the SUV brake hard at the end of the driveway then barrel out into the road.

One of the remaining men asked, "Do we go after her, sir?"

"No need. I always know where to find her. Blood calls blood."

Dominique looked to his fallen man, a pulpy mess on the

ground where Amanda had mutilated then squished him. Again, he smiled.

"Clean this mess and start dismantling the gate for transport," Dominique commanded. "The equipment should be here soon. Search the house and take everything, and I do mean everything, of value. There needs to be no trace left of Randall or his reprobates, you understand?"

He watched as his men scrambled to do his bidding.

"And when we have the gate, and the place is clean, burn it to the ground."

THANK YOU FOR READING!

We want to welcome you to join our newsletter! Be in the know about our upcoming titles and ARC opportunities, discounts and upcoming sales before anyone else!

Find it on: fyresydepublishing.com

Also, feel free to leave a review on Goodreads and your favorite online retailer to tell the author what you thought!

Be sure to join JC Rudkin's personal newsletter and follow them on all their social media!

ABOUT THE AUTHOR

JC Rudkin is the writing team of James and Casey Rudkin. Fans of pulp stories, HP Lovecraft, and modern urban fantasy, they are also role-players and board gamers from back when D&D came in a red box. Their previous collaborations include academic articles, pulp horror short stories, and two daughters. They live in the Upper Peninsula of Michigan where they often have to shovel more than 20 feet of snow each winter.

https://jcrudkin.com/

ACKNOWLEDGMENTS

We would like to thank our family for their unwavering support, especially Zobeida Rudkin, who is very enthusiastic about our writing. We would like to thank our friends, many of whom have gamed with us well into late nights and early mornings, crafting stories and adventures in myriad worlds. We would like to thank Mollie Messick and Boudicca Rudkin for their time and thoughtful suggestions after reading our initial manuscript. And finally, we would like to thank Dr. Diane Keranen of the Word Hell Writers for her insights, encouragement, and invaluable advice. Word Hell Writers 5evah!

When Kira Lockwood meets Blake Michaelson, her perfect life is thrown into the world of chaotic darkness where warlocks desire a slumbering power within her; but will Kira win Blake's heart before he steals her power on her 21st birthday?

Lightning Source UK Ltd.
Milton Keynes UK
UKHW040726240621
386081UK00001B/90

9 780578 936352